'This Isn't V...
Sh...

She should put a stop...

'This isn't business.' ...

'This visit is business,' she protested, trying to gather her wits about her when truly all she wanted to do was fling herself into his arms and find out how his kisses tasted.

'No, it's an exploration.' He threaded his fingers through the wavy mass of her hair and pulled her face close to his. 'You're on an exploration to learn more about ranches in Colorado.'

'Am I on an exploration to learn other things, too?' she asked breathlessly, her gaze dropping to his lips.

'Maybe.' With that he closed the distance between them...

Dear Reader

So Christmas is finally here! We hope you're having a good one and that you're not too busy to enjoy your favourite Desires™.

Let's start with two wonderful books from authors who just don't write often enough! Jennifer Greene has won numerous awards for her writing and this time she brings us **Man of the Month**, Flynn McGannon, who finds *A Baby in His In-Box*. This one is guaranteed to have you laughing! And from another award-winning author, Caroline Cross, comes a super-sexy marriage of convenience story. You won't be able to resist her delicious bad boy, Eli Wilder!

And, no, we haven't forgotten what time of year it is! The Malone family are having *The Best Little Joeville Christmas* in the second book in Anne Eames's trilogy. While Casey Oakes thinks she's going to have the worst Christmas ever, until she becomes *The Surprise Christmas Bride*!

To round off the month, Barbara McMahon brings us a rugged rancher who likes to get his way. And Christine Pacheco's heroine finds *A Husband in Her Stocking* — well, nearly!

Happy reading

The Editors

Santa Cowboy

BARBARA McMAHON

SILHOUETTE

Desire®

*First published in Great Britain 1998
Silhouette Books, Eton House, 18-24 Paradise Road,
Richmond, Surrey TW9 1SR*

© Barbara McMahon 1997

ISBN 0 373 76116 3

22-9812

*Printed and bound in Spain
by Litografia Rosés S.A., Barcelona*

BARBARA McMAHON

was born and raised in the South of the U.S.A. She travelled around the world while working for an international airline, then settled down to raise a family and work for a computer firm. She began writing when her children started school. Now that she has been fortunate enough to realize her long-held dream of quitting her 'day job' and writing full-time, she and her husband have moved from the San Francisco Bay Area to the Sierra Nevada of California. With the beauty of the mountains visible from her windows, and the pace of life slower, she finds more time than ever to think up stories and share them with others. Barbara also writes for Mills & Boon Enchanted®.

Other novels by Barbara McMahon

Silhouette Desire®

One Stubborn Cowboy
Cowboy's Bride
Bride of a Thousand Days
Boss Lady and the Hired Hand

To Michael, who makes it Christmas all year long!

One

"**Y**ou've got the Lone Ranger outside demanding to see you. And if he's not bringing trouble with a capital T, I don't know anything about men," Annalise said dramatically.

For a moment Deb stared at her secretary. Annalise dated more than anyone she knew. The younger woman didn't wait for weekends, she went out five or six times a week, a different man each time. So Annalise knew men, Deb thought. She also knew her boss was working on an important analysis and didn't want to be interrupted. Slowly, Deb put down her pencil and rolled her shoulders to ease the strain.

"The Lone Ranger?" she queried gently.

"Or close kin. Tough, no nonsense. He asked to see you and when I said you were busy, he got really quiet and leaned over my desk, stared me right in the eyes and said he would wait until you weren't busy, but he would damn well see you today. Sent shivers up my spine, I can tell you." Annalise smiled smugly. "Of course, he's a hunk and a half. I wouldn't mind him waiting all day out there until you can see him. I'd be glad to keep an eye on him. But I don't think he's going to be easy to get rid of."

Deb frowned and stood. Slowly, she walked toward the door. "Did he say why he wanted to see me? What about?"

"No." Her excitement almost tangible, Annalise stepped to one side as Deb reached for the doorknob.

Feeling like a kid again, Deb eased the door away from the frame enough to peek through the opening. The man stood with feet braced, twisting a Stetson in his hand. He did look a bit like the Lone Ranger—tall, rugged, forceful. Only he wore no mask—which was probably good, since this was a bank and wearing a mask could prove dangerous. Did he represent truth, justice and the American way? She frowned, maybe that was Superman, not the Lone Ranger.

In reality, he looked like a rangy cowboy, all jeans, muscles, angular features and testosterone. Deb often saw men like him strutting down the streets of Denver. She avoided them whenever possible. They came from a different world than she— one so foreign to her she never considered venturing in.

She closed the door and looked at Annalise. One thing was for sure, Annalise had been right about his being a hunk. Keeping her demeanor calm with some effort, Deb slowly moved back to her desk.

"Since my concentration's been broken, I'll take a break and see him. If he hasn't left in ten minutes, call in and say I have an important call," Deb instructed.

"Gotcha." Annalise smiled and eagerly turned to leave.

Deb sank behind her desk, thankful for its formidable size, feeling she'd need the distance for the coming confrontation. Who was her visitor and what did he want? The bank president liked sending irate customers to her because of her ability to soothe them out of temper and smooth over the business relationship. It didn't matter to him that she hated that part of her job, or that she often wondered why her co-worker Phil Moore never had to do that kind of work. Though she knew her boss played favorites, Deb was helpless to do anything about it. She was bucking for a vice presidency and would not jeopardize her chances by appearing to be anything less than a team player. She gritted her teeth each time and did her best.

She could handle the rangy cowboy. He hadn't really looked angry, just resolute. And tall. And big. And very male. She straightened the spreadsheet and waited for him to enter. She'd hear him out, attempt to solve whatever had brought him here, get rid of him, and get back to her analysis.

"Are you D. Harrington? I expected a man." The deep voice at the door drew her attention, and her eyes widened. Closer, he appeared stunning. His eyes were a bright blue, like the clear sky over Denver on a summer's day. His angular features suggested a face that looked as if it had been carved from brown sandstone. His strong jaw looked stubborn and determined. She would bet the bank he would have waited all day to see her just as he'd said.

His broad shoulders were encased in a sheepskin-lined denim jacket. While not new, the jacket appeared newer than the faded jeans that clad his long muscular legs. And both looked in better shape than the scuffed and dusty boots. Had he just ridden in off the range? For one foolish moment she wondered if he had a horse tied outside. Deb shook her head slightly at the absurdity. Annoyingly, her heart pounded as she took in every inch of him. Stalling for a moment until her heart rate slowed, she swallowed and let her eyes trace over him as she raised her gaze to meet his.

Slowly, because courtesy demanded it, for no other reason, Deb rose and offered her hand. She couldn't help it if he thought D. Harrington was a man. "D for Deb. And you are…"

He stepped into her office and pushed the door closed behind him. Before it had a chance to click shut, he'd crossed the room to stand near her desk, dropped the Stetson on one chair, hooked the second one closer with his boot and sank down upon it, ignoring her outstreched hand. His hard glare never wavered from her face.

"My name won't mean much to you. I'm Dusty Wilson. I'm here on behalf of John Barrett."

Deb sat, straightened the folders to the left of the spreadsheet and glanced at the man. "I don't discuss customer's affairs with others. If Mr. Barrett needs to discuss his situation, he can do so himself."

"That he can't do. He's been ill and is still bedridden."

She blinked. "I didn't realize that."

"That much is obvious. If you or anyone else in this bank had the common decency to call and find out what was going on, you would have discovered the facts. But everything's been done by mail, and by the book. You can't foreclose on the property."

She bristled. "Now wait a minute. We tried to contact him, by letter and phone. We received no response. He's months in arrears, if I remember correctly. If Mr. Barrett doesn't clear the indebtedness by the date stated in the letter, we have no choice but to proceed under the full extent of the law."

She itched to refresh her memory with the Barrett folder. The successful resolution of this account would go a long way toward cementing her chances for that vice presidency. Reluctant to instigate foreclosure proceedings, she'd had no other choice once the president began to hint that perhaps she wasn't up to the task of keeping her accounts in order. She'd continually attempted to reach John Barrett as she'd followed procedures in great detail, to make sure every step taken complied with the law. She had stalled as long as she could. Then, to prove to the president and the members of the board of directors that a woman was perfectly capable of handling the added responsibilities of the position of vice president, no matter how difficult those tasks were, she'd finally initiated the formal steps.

Staring at the man sitting opposite her, Deb vowed she would not let some yahoo cowboy jeopardize her promotion.

He didn't reply immediately, instead his gaze traveled insolently over her, from the tip of her head to where the edge of the desk blocked his view. For one stunning moment Deb wanted to reach up to make sure her hair was neat and in place. She blinked, heat rising in her cheeks. Usually she didn't care what she looked like, beyond conveying a professional demeanor. The suit colors she wore indicated she knew what was proper for a banking environment: dark blue, charcoal gray, black. She certainly didn't care what some stranger thought of her appearance.

So why did her heart pound? Why did she long to take off her jacket to ease the heat that enveloped her? Why did she feel curiously aware of him? Her senses were attuned to his breathing, his strength, his masculinity. Every beat of her heart made her that much more aware.

Good Lord! What was the matter with her? He was just another irate customer she needed to placate. It was part of her job.

"Play Scrooge some other time. It won't hurt you to hold off on your blasted foreclosure for a few months. You can't sell the property right away anyway, land values are way down and nothing moves at Christmas. In a few months John'll be back on his feet. Once he musters some cattle, sells them, he'll be good for the money."

"We don't work that way, Mr.—" Horrified she stared at him. She never forgot names. But she could only remember his first name. Dusty. And that because she'd wondered briefly if his name came from the dust on his boots. How could she forget his last name? She knew color stained her cheeks, but her mind remained a blank. This never happened. She prided herself on her professionalism. Just because his perusal shook her to her core was no reason to draw a blank.

Taking a breath, she tried to recapture control of the discussion. Tried to ignore the fact that he made her nervous. Tried to ignore the odd reaction churning inside as he stared at her. His eyes were so blue, and seemed to see everything—even how nervous he made her.

She knew he knew it when the left side of his mouth slowly moved up in a half derisive, lopsided smile. His eyes danced with amusement as he remained quiet, waiting to see how she dug herself out of this hole. Undoubtedly enjoying her discomfort as the seconds ticked by, he did nothing to help her out, which made Deb even more determined to take charge of the conversation.

Taking a deep breath, she began to speak in a reasonable

tone, as if lecturing a five-year-old. "The bank has certain rules it follows. We can't extend indefinite credit to everyone or we would be out of business in no time. Mr. Barrett knew the terms when he signed the agreement. He has not followed them. As for being close to Christmas, we have been trying for months to contact him. Had he paid like he was supposed to, we wouldn't have this problem. We are within our rights—"

"Rights be damned. We're talking about a man who has worked his entire life on this ranch. Now he's run into a spot of trouble. The least you can do is give him a chance to explain things, to see if some compromise can be worked out."

"We tried!" Deb resented this man's implications. If only he knew the trouble she'd risked by delaying as long as she had. Her boss already watched her every move on this deal. Who did this man think he was to come in and accuse her of rushing?

Dusty Wilson rose, looming over her desk and leaning on the edge with his powerful fists. Deb leaned back in her chair. He stood three feet away, but she felt overwhelmed by his presence. His eyes grew stormy, and piercing, as if he could see down to her soul, and didn't like what he saw. His big body filled her vision, his denim as out of place in her pristine office as her silk blouse would be on his ranch. The power he radiated enveloped her, kept her silent as she watched, fascinated, to see his next move. She could no more have captured control of the encounter than she could ride a bucking horse. Blood rushed through her veins as she filled her eyes with him.

"Your name was on the letter, D. Harrington. But you are not the only employee at the bank. I'll talk to the president and see if I can make him see sense. If not, I have a few friends at the Denver *Free Press*. Maybe a human interest story about the big bad corporate bank ruining a small-time rancher without any regard for the man's illness and temporary situation will garner some interest. Maybe another bank will even step in and assume the debt, becoming a hero to a million depositors." He reached for his hat and turned to leave.

"Wait." A touch of panic coursed through her. The last thing Deb wanted was for him to go to the president. Josiah Montgomery was not shy about making his opinions about women in banking known. She often thought he tolerated her because of the changing views of board members toward women in business. In her heart, she knew he would relish any opportunity to keep her from the vice presidency. But her past performance had been exemplary. She'd worked too long and too hard for that spot to risk it because of some loud-mouthed cowboy riding a grudge.

To make matters worse, this rowdy cowboy was just the kind of good ole boy Josiah Montgomery liked to hobnob with. Her boss would delight in the two of them joining forces against the little woman. He would side with this man on general principles alone, with no consideration to the validity of his claim. She couldn't allow that.

Deb gritted her teeth as the cowboy turned and raised an eyebrow. "Please sit back down Mr.—" Damn, what *was* his name?

"Wilson, ma'am. It's Dusty Wilson," he said, as if talking to an idiot.

"I'm sorry, Mr. Wilson. Please sit back down and let's discuss this just a bit. I can explain the bank's position and maybe—"

"I already know the bank's position. I'm here to see what we can do to change it." He didn't move from the door.

"I'll review the case and see if there is anything we can do. Maybe an extension, though I believe we already granted a couple." She wished she had the folder with her.

The phone rang.

"Excuse me," she mumbled, dropping her gaze from his. Deb picked up the phone. Her fingers shook a bit as she frowned. She would not let this man upset her. She was good at her job, she could handle this—if he would just sit down and stop looming! "Deb Harrington."

"You have an important call," Annalise said.

"Ask them to call back, please. And could you bring me

the Barrett file?'' Deb said, her eyes darting to her visitor. He remained by the door. She swallowed hard.

"I thought you wanted to be interrupted so you could get rid of Mr. Hunk," Annalise said.

"Just bring the folder." Deb hung up and glanced at the spreadsheet on her desk. She had wanted to finish her analysis this morning. A nice quiet exercise in making sure the numbers matched. She hated it when plans got disrupted. Straightening her shoulders, she raised her head. The price of success. She would not bemoan it. It was what she wanted, had worked for over the last few years.

"My secretary will bring in the folder and I'll see what I can do," she said.

Slowly, Dusty Wilson nodded and moved to sit in the chair, resting his hat on his knee. He looked out the window. Ms. Harrington had a corner office with a view of the front range of the Rockies. Early snow capped the distant peaks, the closer hills were tree-covered and green. He wondered how often the uptight Ms. Harrington stared out the window. Wondered if she ever stopped work long enough to appreciate the beauty of the scene, if it gave her any serenity during the day.

Or was she too caught up in squeezing customers who were a bit late in paying on loans, disregarding the reasons, gleefully rubbing her hands in delight at yet another foreclosure? He glanced at her again. She was the image of Marjory. Not in a physical sense. Her honey-blond hair looked nothing like Marjory's sleek, dark red bob, but both styles were severe. Marjory's had been short. This woman had her hair dragged ruthlessly back into some sort of knot at the base of her neck. The tailored bow that clipped it did nothing to ease the severity. Her makeup was flawless. Her suit stylish and fitted. She appeared to be the epitome of a successful female executive.

For a second Dusty wondered if she was as consumed with the corporate game as Marjory had been. Of course she was. One look at her was enough to tell him that. And despite the momentary flash of awareness that surprised him when he first saw her, he wanted nothing to do with her. If he could get a reprieve for John, he'd be finished. No matter how sexy the stiff Ms. Harrington looked, he'd tried a relationship with a fast-track woman once before. He'd thought it exhilarating at first, the power that Marjory wielded, the goals she'd set, her outgunning of the men she worked with. But that was before he'd been burned. Now he wanted his women soft and sweet and interested in him, not fascinated in bottom lines and profit margins.

The last type he'd ever fall for again would be *Ms*. D. Harrington.

When the door opened, he looked around at the secretary. Now there was a handful, unless he missed his guess. His eyes met hers and he smiled in reply to the flash of her white teeth. She was so busy giving him the eye, she almost missed that massive desk. She looked soft and pretty and flirted like a cowboy's dream. If he had any thoughts about women, which he didn't, he'd center them on this young lady rather than the witch behind the desk. But he had come on John's behalf. He'd get business settled and be on his way.

"Thank you, Annalise. That's all."

Even her voice sounded cool as ice. He looked at the woman behind the desk, betting she was frozen through and through. Maybe an annual report got her blood pumping, but he bet nothing short of that would. For a moment he wondered what would happen if he kissed her. Would his lips freeze, or would she thaw for a split second? Would those violet eyes widen in surprise, or would she stare through him in disgust as if he were red ink?

He smiled grimly as she opened the folder, stared at it for a long minute, almost as if seeking something that would help her out of this tight spot. He had started here with her, but he would make good his promise. If she didn't help him out, he'd move on up the ladder of the bank. If he still didn't find satisfaction, he'd hit the press. What they were doing just wasn't right. John was too sick to fight it, but he wasn't.

She cleared her throat nervously. Dusty felt something ease. He made her nervous. Good, dammit. She deserved it for all she'd put John through.

Deb looked up. "We've been more than fair with Mr. Barrett. He's over six months in arrears." She picked up half a dozen sheets of paper. "We've written many times. I have copies of all the letters. And the phone log, apparently he has no answering machine, yet we tried to reach him many times. There's been no effort made to pay—"

"He's been sick. Things have slid, but we can straighten it all out. We just need some time."

"We should have been approached when this first became a problem. In situations like this it is usually easier—"

"I just found out about it yesterday." He pulled a folded paper from his pocket and tossed it contemptuously on her desk. "Your notice to pay in full or vacate the property immediately. We need more time."

"I can't see how he's going to come up with the money if he's so delinquent."

"You hold the mortgage on the property to cover any possible losses. We're asking for a couple more weeks. In that time John's friends can rally around and make the payments. He'll be good for it. We trust him."

"Sound like something from *It's a Wonderful Life*," she murmured.

Dusty raised his eyebrows. What would this hard-nosed businesswoman know about a sloppy romantic film like *It's a Wonderful Life?* He looked closely at her. For a moment he wondered if she'd created a facade for the bank. Was she a closet romantic? He almost laughed at the notion. She was hard as rock, and as inflexible. Thinking differently made *him* the romantic.

"Some people do make friends in this life, Ms. Harrington, not enemies. You probably didn't realize that," he drawled.

Startled at the stab of pain his words evoked, Deb stared at him. What could she say to wipe that nasty lopsided grin off his face? What could she do to get rid of the man and never have to see him again?

"We're discussing business, Mr. Wilson, not social standing. If you were a depositor in our bank, would you like to wait six months to get any interest due your account? In essence, that's what you're asking—delay paying our depositors because one man can't keep his loan payments current. We'd go out of business in a heartbeat if we allowed things like that to continue.''

''It's all just numbers to you, isn't it?'' he asked softly.

''I have certain responsibilities—''

''Responsibilities be hanged. For once, think like a human being. Give a little thought to the hardship of the people who do business with your bank, then cut them some slack. It'll do more for your bank than anything.''

Deb clenched her hands, dropping them in her lap so he couldn't see the action. Was this cowboy trying to tell her how to do her job?

''You do know ranchers aren't like bankers, don't you? They don't have money coming in each week in a paycheck, neatly filled out with all the deductions taken. They get money in lumps when they sell hay or cattle. They pay it out as demanded, sometimes borrowing against future income just because the money flow isn't consistent.''

''I don't need a lesson on ranch economics,'' she said dryly, swallowing to ease the tightness in her throat. She knew how ranchers ran their business. John Barrett had been typical, his strong economic record qualifying him for advantageous loan rates.

''When was the last time you were on a ranch?'' Dusty asked, feeling his exasperation grow. He was getting nowhere with the buttoned-up banker. If something didn't kick loose soon, he'd give up and move on to the president.

His question surprised her, he could tell by her expression.

''I've never been on a ranch.''

''What? A good half or more of your business comes from the ranchers who live around here. You've never bothered to go out and see any of them?''

''We don't make house calls,'' she replied stiffly.

''Yet you're planning to jerk John's ranch out from under him. Sell it to the highest bidder. And you've never even seen the property. How do you know you'd be getting a fair price?''

''As long as the realty company we hire sells the property

for at least the amount of the loan, I don't need to know any more. Any additional funds would be sent to Mr. Barrett. I have neither the time nor the inclination to be running around to every problem account we have to see what we can do to accommodate late payments.'' She didn't like the stand she had taken, but it was business. Surely he could understand that.

Dusty rose and clapped his hat on his head. He stared at the woman for a long moment, catching a glimpse of uncertainty in her violet eyes. Damn, why couldn't she have stringy hair and dull eyes and a wart on her nose? No, she had to be a looker. For a moment he wished he'd met her at the Rustler's Roost on Friday night. Maybe after they shared a dance or two, a kiss or two, he'd forget her as he did most women.

She was too citified for him to contend with on a long-term basis. But he was loco if he thought she'd ever show up at a honky-tonk like Rustler's.

"I'm out of here. I'll take this up with Josiah Montgomery." He turned and had the door open before she could react.

"Please. Mr. Wilson, wait." Scrambling around her desk, practically running across the office, Deb reached out and grabbed his arm.

Dusty glanced down at the pale hand, noting how small it seemed against his arm. How perfectly the oval nails had been polished. Then he looked at her. She barely reached his shoulder. He could easily look down on the top of her head. Small package to contain such a threat to one of his old friends.

Small, but shapely. The fragrance that seemed to come from her was light, sweet and innocent.

Damn. He didn't need this sexual awareness of the woman. She represented the enemy, pure and simple. And he didn't like the stirring of interest in his body. Time to find someone to ease his ache, and this woman was not in the running.

She was a fighter, he'd give her that. Smiling grimly, she didn't let go of his arm. She was trying to recover the ground that seemed to be slipping away. He waited, curious about what she'd say now.

"Mr. Montgomery depends on me to handle things of this

nature. I'm sure if we just discuss it a bit more we can come to an equitable agreement.''

''I'll tell you what, Ms. Harrington, you come to the Circle B with me, talk to John directly, and then see if you can come up with some sort of compromise. In the meantime, I'll contact some of John's friends and see how much money we can raise to tide him over.''

She hesitated. He could almost see the wheels turning in her mind. Weighing the different options. He knew how she thought, and didn't like it. So, would she take a chance and come out with him, or stick to her prim little office with her rules and regulations?

''How long would it take?'' she asked.

Slowly, Dusty smiled in triumph. She was coming out to the ranch with him.

''Well, ma'am, it's a good two-hour ride from here. You'll want to see it all and then talk with John. You'll need to know that he runs a good spread and is good for the money. Then it'll take me a while to contact everyone who would want to help him out. Maybe a day. Maybe longer.''

''A day! I can't be gone from work for an entire day!''

''Day after tomorrow is Saturday, so you wouldn't be taking time from work. We could go up tomorrow night, so you could see the ranch at sunrise on Saturday. It's a pretty location.''

''Sunrise?'' she said faintly.

Dusty cleared his throat to conceal his need to laugh at her expression. Didn't she know there was a sunrise every morning? Did she always wake up when the sun was already high in the sky? He'd like to get Miss Executive to the ranch, show her a few things, knock that chip off her shoulder. At the very least have her see John as a regular human being, not some statistic or sheet of numbers in a folder.

And maybe see what happened if he kissed her? The thought came insidiously.

''Do you need anything, Ms. Harrington?'' Annalise asked from her desk, eyeing the two in the doorway with rampant curiosity.

"No." Tugging on his arm, she pulled Dusty back into her office and closed the door. "Mr. Wilson—"

"You might as well call me Dusty, since we'll be spending the weekend together," he interrupted, amusement starting to build. He'd like to take this lady down a peg or two. Not just for John. She rubbed him the wrong way—and reminded him too much of Marjory.

"Dusty, then. I could probably drive out for a quick look on Saturday. If you would give me the directions. What time would be good?"

"Your best bet is to come with me. I've got a sturdy truck. You probably drive some sissy sports car."

She drew herself up and glared at him. "I may drive a sports car but it's not a sissy car."

Just the kind of flashy statement Marjory used to make. "Conspicuous consumption," he murmured. Do whatever it took to make sure everyone knew how much money she made, how successful she was.

Deb smiled at him. There was so much ice in the look he almost shivered.

"The car is twelve years old. And I live in fear it'll die one day, especially now, in the dead of winter. Not that it's any of your business. I don't need to visit the ranch overnight. Pick me up Saturday morning." Turning, she moved nearer her desk, as if it were a talisman.

Dusty wasn't standing for any of her boss-lady orders. "I'm leaving tomorrow at 6:00 p.m. sharp. If you're coming, you'll be ready. I'll have you home in time for work on Monday."

"What?" She spun around and stared at him in horror. "That's the entire weekend. I can't go for the entire weekend. I agreed to look at the stupid ranch, not move in!"

"Important personal plans, sweetheart?" he asked silkily.

"I'm not your sweetheart! This is business."

"My guess is you aren't any man's sweetheart. If you want to drive yourself, fine. I'll swing by at six tomorrow. If you go with me, you'll be ready. Otherwise, I'll tell John to expect you sometime Saturday. *Late* Saturday, probably." His tone left no doubt what he thought.

Incensed and uncertain, Deb was so mixed up she didn't know what to say next. He hurt her. He couldn't know the pain his scathing words caused and she'd die before she'd give him half a clue. She didn't know whether to try to prove him wrong or to quietly sneak away and leave him the battlefield.

Battle? He was trying to help a friend. And that earlier remark of his had cut, as well. She *did* have friends. Maybe she wasn't as close to them as John sounded to Dusty. Suddenly she couldn't imagine any of her friends rallying around her if she needed help. But she could spend quiet evenings together with her friends every few months. Even go skiing on occasion.

She had overcome tremendous odds to get where she was—though she kept that a closely guarded secret. It was her life and she liked it just fine the way it was. She had everything planned. The next step would be the vice presidency. Then maybe it would be time to find a mate. But right now she had to concentrate on her job. She was too close to achieving all she wanted to let anything stand in her way.

He watched her like a hawk. Deb wished he'd never showed up. Wished she had not agreed to see him. He was as tenacious as a bulldog. And she didn't like the amusement that lurked in his eyes. She was not the butt of some joke, but a professional woman doing a tough job to the best of her ability. Time he remembered it.

"If you could bring me home Saturday, I'd be able to leave tomorrow night," she said with as much dignity as she could muster. She had to look away from those compelling eyes. She wondered what it would feel like to have them hot with passion when looking at her, instead of regarding her with amusement or disdain. Where had *that* thought come from?

"Look on it as a minivacation. You do take vacations, don't you?" he drawled. At her abrupt nod, he grinned. "Some people pay a fortune to spend a week at a working ranch. You'll get a weekend for free."

"I need to be home Sunday," she said firmly. Her idea of a vacation was a week on the beach at Cancun, not some working ranch, especially in late November. Was it covered in snow? It had been a dry fall in Denver, but she didn't how the weather had been in the outlying hills.

"Can't promise that. I have a spread of my own to run, and I need to see what help John needs. Of course, if you help out with chores, it'll make the work go that much faster and we can get away earlier."

"I know nothing about cattle," she said stiffly. What was she getting herself into? She was supposed to be going just to look at the property, not work as a cowhand.

"Oh, honey, there's plenty to do on a ranch that has nothing to do with cattle. But not dressed like you're dressed. Wear jeans. I suppose it's too much to hope you have some boots."

"No, I don't have boots," she snapped, feeling that uncertain pull of attraction as his eyes roamed over her. No one had ever called her "honey" before. She didn't like it. She frowned, wanting to be thought of for her business acumen, not her femininity. Yet every time he looked at her, really looked at her, she felt like a woman. A wanton woman needing nothing more than for a man to admire her. Maybe more than admire her. Desire her. She drew in a breath, afraid to continue thinking along those lines.

Good grief, was she going through some midlife crisis? She wasn't even thirty yet.

For a moment Dusty's eyes traced every inch of her. She'd look mighty fine in jeans—tight ones that molded those sweet hips and tucked into that narrow waist. If she wore a button shirt, starchy like her blouse, he'd wish it was summer so riding would make her warm enough to unfasten some of those buttons. He bet her skin was milky white all over. No tan because she took no time for outdoor play, she was all work.

Then the fanciful notion struck him that late November might be the best month, after all. It was cold on the ranch, maybe she'd need to snuggle up against him for warmth. If she reached up her arms to encircle his neck, she'd stretch out that lovely little body against his and fit just right, he bet. He could even pick her up; she couldn't weigh more than a hundred pounds soaking wet.

Dusty drew in a sharp breath and started for the door. He

would not think about that feminine body naked and wet, her hair swirling around her face instead of tied back, those violet eyes gazing at him in wonder and desire. He'd been down that road once before. Never again.

"Tomorrow at six," he growled as he flung the door wide and stormed through it. By this time tomorrow he had better get his head on straight and remember why he was taking Ms. Deb Harrington away for the weekend or there'd be hell to pay.

Two

Deb shoved the hangers as far to the left as she could get them, peering into the darkest corner of her closet. Somewhere she had a pair of jeans. She knew she did. It had been years since she'd worn them, but she never threw anything away. She pushed an old dress aside. Darn, why didn't she get some kind of light installed in the closet? She could see a lot better if—ah, there they were. Yanking the old denim from the hanger, she stepped back into her bedroom and held them up triumphantly.

Glancing at the clock, she drew in a breath and began to throw off her business clothes. Dusty Wilson would arrive in ten minutes. She still had to decide what to take for the weekend. She had a few casual tops, they would do. Tossing her camisole aside, she opened the drawer and rummaged around. The yellow turtleneck; she looked good in yellow. She pulled it on. Picking up two more sweaters, she tossed them onto the bed. That would do for tomorrow. And one extra just in case.

Rummaging in her sock drawer, she withdrew three thick pairs. She didn't have boots, but she did have sneakers. For

BARBARA McMAHON 25

an instant the image of Dusty Wilson's mocking gaze danced before her eyes. She pressed her lips together tightly. Not everyone had cowboy boots. She wasn't a cowboy, had no intentions of ever becoming one. So why would she buy boots?

She pulled on the jeans. Gosh, she didn't remember them being so tight. Tugging the zipper, it scarcely moved. A quick glance at the clock showed her she had seven minutes. Certainly no time to find a store and buy a new pair.

"And there is no way I'm not going to be wearing jeans when that smug, self-satisfied, know-it-all cowboy shows up!" she vowed.

She flung herself back on her bed, sucked in and slid the zipper up. Slowly she exhaled, staring at the ceiling, wondering if she had lost her mind.

"I can't believe I got talked into going to a ranch for the weekend. I don't need to see a ranch to know whether to lend money or not. An applicant's credit record is more important. And I should drive myself. That way, if things get awkward, I can leave," she mumbled. Pushing herself upright, she glanced down. The faded blue denim jeans were skintight, revealing every curve. Gingerly she walked around the room, leaning over and stretching them out. They would loosen, she was sure of it. They had to; she didn't have another pair and there was no way she would have Dusty—Mr. Wilson—show up and find her in anything else.

Not that she cared what he thought. But if she was to gain any credibility in his eyes, he had to stop criticizing her long enough to pay attention to what she had to say.

When the knock came a few moments later, Deb was as ready as she ever would be. Her small overnight case stood by the door. Her warm jacket lay across it. She'd watered her plants, turned her light timer on and closed her bedroom door to the turmoil in her room. She'd put her clothes away on Sunday.

Opening the door, Deb stared. Over the few hours since she'd seen him yesterday she'd forgotten how tall he stood. Forgotten how his eyes pierced her, how his face seemed hewn from solid rock, how that smile tripped her heart. Forgotten how sexy—

Sexy? Oh, she did need a break. This man had threatened her very job—there was nothing sexy about that. Not that he looked threatening at the moment, unless it was to her equilibrium. He slouched against the doorjamb, wearing the same jacket as yesterday, his hat held in his hands. That half lopsided smile lit his face and his blue eyes stared into hers with intensity. His dark hair was thick with just a hint of a wave.

Deb's heart rate sped up. She swallowed, desperate for the calm that she usually mustered in awkward situations. "I'm ready," she said brightly, unable to look away. Heat rose in her cheeks and she licked suddenly dry lips. She was almost thirty years old and felt like a shy schoolgirl with a crush on the football hero. Had Dusty played football? He had the shoulders for it. And the long legs that could have carried the winning touchdown.

"I like promptness in a woman." His voice came soft and slow, like a lover's seductive caress in the dark of midnight.

Wondering what else he liked in a woman, she dragged her gaze away with almost physical effort. He looked as if he'd lean against the jamb all night. She thought he'd wanted to hurry to get to his friend's place. "Promptness is a virtue in all business situations," she said primly. She knew time represented money.

"Is that a fact?" he asked. "You paint those jeans on?" The sexy Western drawl made the question all the more intimate, all the more suggestive.

Deb blinked and shook her head as embarrassment rushed through her. She knew the jeans were too tight. "You said wear jeans."

"You give a whole new meaning to the word, sweetcakes. I'm not complaining. Far from it." His grin was pure male appreciation.

Deb drew herself up to her full five feet four inches and tilted her head back. She wished she could match his height; he had to be a bit over six feet. It would be great to be able to look down on him—and find some clever phrase that would put him in his place. She had not worn jeans to invite some lascivious remark from a woman-hungry cowboy. She wished now that she'd worn her brown wool slacks. They were comfortable and certainly nowhere near as tight as these pants. But then he would have mocked her for lack of jeans.

Before any scathing words came to mind, Dusty gestured to her small suitcase. "That all you're taking?"

"Yes."

"I'm surprised you're traveling so light. My wife used to take three or four bags anytime she went anywhere." Running his fingers through his hair, he placed his hat on his head before reaching for the case. He held out her jacket.

He was married? Disappointment pierced her as she shrugged into the sleeves. Not that she cared. In fact, it was a very *good* thing. She could not be tempted by a married man. It no longer mattered that he looked like a gift from the gods. So what if dark hair and blue eyes were a killer combination? And who even cared that his lopsided smiles melted something inside her each time he aimed one her way? Maybe his wife cared, but not Deb. And she could just stop thinking about midnights and caresses and seduction.

Glad to have it all settled, Deb felt better about the venture. She liked to know the boundaries and playing field. Emotions did not go with business. Taking her briefcase, she glanced around, feeling oddly confused. She should be staying home and enjoying her free weekend, not traipsing off to some ranch.

"You're taking that?" he asked, cocking one eyebrow, her overnight case easily held as if it weighed nothing.

"Of course. This is a business trip, right? I have Mr. Barrett's folder."

"As well as a few other cases you're handling, I bet." His tone had grown decidedly colder.

"Actually, I'm only bringing his folder. I don't work every weekend if I can help it." Not anymore, anyway.

"No pushing to get ahead by doing more work than expected?" he asked stepping aside so she could move out onto the stoop.

Deb pulled the door shut, disturbed by his closeness. Why
didn't he step back? She checked the knob, reluctant to turn
around. If he didn't move, she would bump right into him.
Even with her back to him, she could feel the heat from his
body, smell the tantalizing mixture of aftershave, leather and
man. A small shiver of excitement curled deep within her.
Ruthlessly she squashed it. This was business, business, business.

"I do my job fine without having to work every weekend."
She'd passed the stage of giving her all. Working smarter, not
harder, had enabled her to claim more free time.

"Thought all career women were the same. My wife used
to work all hours of the night and weekends."

"Used to? Has she now reached the stage where she no
longer has to work so many hours?" she asked, turning
around. He'd stepped away. He wasn't as close as she had
thought, thank goodness. Taking a breath, Deb decided maybe
she did need a break, she was imagining things.

Dusty stepped off the stoop and led the way to an old pickup
parked at the curb. "I don't know or care. We're divorced."

Deb stumbled but quickly recovered. He was divorced? *Single?*

"How long ago?" she blurted without thought. How could
he be free to roam around looking as good as he did? Were
the other women of Colorado blind? Not that she would be
interested in some cocky cowboy, but she knew from Annalise
and others that many women found such men fascinating. Annoyed that she was spending so much time thinking about him,
Deb quickly determined that she'd check out the situation with
John Barrett then ask to be returned home.

Dusty tossed her case into the bed of the truck and leaned
against the side as she walked toward him. One finger pushed
back his hat and his blue eyes seemed brighter than ever. Deb
warily stopped a few feet away. Would he open the door for
her or wait for her to do it herself? Did she want to brush past
that body to get into the truck?

"Three years, four months and seventeen days," he said.

"But who's counting?" she replied, uncertain by the exactness of the response. Did he regret it? Did he still carry a torch for the woman? Some strong emotion must play into this, for him to be so exact in his answer.

"Not counting, celebrating. Every day without Marjory is a celebration." He opened the door with his left hand, not moving from his position against the side of the truck. "Let's go. We have Denver traffic to clear before we get on the open road."

Deb had to brush by him to reach the seat. She clambered in without assistance, only to have the door slammed shut before she settled. Her eyes tracked Dusty as he rounded the front of the truck and opened his own door.

"How did you get the name Dusty?" she asked when he started the engine. There were a hundred questions she wanted answers to, but she'd start with the simple, noninvolved ones. It was pure curiosity, nothing more.

He grinned and gunned the engine. The truck pulled into traffic. "My full name is William Dustin Wilson. My dad's Will, so my folks called me Dusty as a kid. It stuck."

"Is your father still alive?"

"Sure, isn't yours?" he asked.

She shook her head. No, he was no longer alive and she was grateful it was so.

"Both my parents are alive and well. Is your mother alive?" he asked.

She shook her head again and looked out the window. She watched the trendy section of Denver flash by, firmly keeping her thoughts away from the past.

"How did you know where to pick me up?" she asked, suddenly remembering she hadn't given him her address. Had it been to avoid the commitment for the weekend?

"Your secretary told me how to find it. I could have checked the phone book, but that was easier."

"I could have driven myself," she said slowly, growing more certain by the minute that going with Dusty Wilson would prove to be a mistake. Maybe the entire trip would prove to be a monumental error of judgment.

"And have your aging car die on the way? I wouldn't want

that on my conscience. Besides, after a tough day foreclosing on people, a hard-hearted banker probably needs to rest up, leave the driving to someone else.''

She flushed and looked at him. His profile was strong, his jaw stubborn and square. His nose had a bump on it, as if it had been broken once. In a fight? Deb could picture him wading in and throwing punches left and right. She felt like throwing a few herself. She didn't need his cutting tongue.

"I don't spend all day foreclosing on people," she said in defense.

He flicked her a glance, teasing glints in his eyes. "Is that right? What do you do?"

"More often than not I'm approving loans, doing what I can to help people. Why didn't your friend respond to our letters or phone calls? We might have cleared this up and made other arrangements months ago." Then I wouldn't need to be in this truck, seated by a sexy cowboy, driving west to see some ranch on the brink of foreclosure.

The space in the cab seemed to grow smaller as she became more aware of Dusty Wilson. His hands were large and brown, gripping the wheel with casual confidence. She glanced at her own hands. How much smaller were they? Would his hand completely engulf hers? Would he have calluses? She knew the muscles beneath his shirt were gained from genuine work, not some gym in town. She had never explored a man's body. Would those muscles feel hard as iron, or pliant beneath her fingers? Would his skin feel hot, or cool? Stretched out side by side, how far below her feet would his legs stretch?

"I told you, he's been sick. His mail's piled up. I picked up the last batch at the post office and saw your final notice stamped on the envelope. I guess he hasn't bothered to answer the phone."

"And in rides the hero," she murmured.

"Got it in one, sweetcakes."

"I am not your sweetheart nor sweetcakes. My name is Deb."

"Short for Deborah?"

"Yes."

"I would think you'd use the full name in your mighty position at the bank."

"I don't denigrate your chosen profession, Mr. Wilson, please refrain from denigrating mine," she said firmly. She liked banking, found satisfaction in working with customers, in putting together deals that benefited everyone. Of course there were aspects she didn't like, but every job had those. Even ranching, she suspected.

"Point taken. My apologies. I'm just mad."

"I can tell, but maybe some of that anger should roll John Barrett's way. If he had made some arrangements about his bills, I wouldn't be here trying to see what kind of compromise we might work out." She still couldn't believe she'd agreed to this visit. Would it change anything?

"Maybe it wasn't all bad, then," Dusty said audaciously, winking at her. "I've got a pretty woman beside me, a weekend ahead of us. What more could a man ask for?"

"A good credit line, for one," she snapped, flustered he had called her pretty. She thought back. Had anyone else ever called her pretty? No one came to mind.

"That's the banker—let nothing come between you and the bottom line. What hobbies do you have, ironing dollar bills?"

She grinned and tried to relax. He was deliberately trying to provoke her and she wasn't sure why. But she did know if one didn't respond to teasing, the teaser stopped.

"I like to crochet, actually," she said.

He looked startled, stared at her for a long moment. Just when she feared they'd crash, he looked back to the roadway.

"Not very high profile, is it?" he asked.

"High profile is for jobs, not hobbies. I'm beginning to detect a trend here. Was your wife by any chance an executive on the fast track?"

"Got it in one, sweetcakes."

Deb ignored the deliberate use of the offensive word and nodded. "And you didn't like her working so hard to get ahead."

He shrugged. "I don't mind hard work. I do a bit myself. What I objected to was her obsession with work, with getting ahead, with beating out the others who stood in her way no matter how she did it.''

"It's harder for a woman to get ahead than a man," she stated.

"It wasn't the getting ahead that bothered me, it was her obsession. And the ostentatious flaunting of each status symbol she acquired."

She studied him for a moment. Rugged and untamed, she could see him on the range, battling nature, and winning more often than not. Material things probably didn't mean much to him. She didn't believe he was one of those men threatened by women who made more money, or achieved greater business success. He came across too self-assured, too confident in his own worth. There was no problem understanding him, but he didn't understand his wife. Ex-wife. And Deb understood perfectly.

"Maybe she just tried to show you she was doing well," she said softly.

"Me and the world. And she didn't show, she rammed it down my throat."

Deb watched the scenery streaming by. They had left Denver behind and were on the freeway heading toward the mountains that filled the horizon. It was not her place to discuss his wife. *Ex*-wife. For a moment she gave some thought to proving to Dusty Wilson that she was nothing like his wife. But the moment passed. There was no reason. Nothing would come of it. Her visit this weekend was to see if she could make a recommendation to delay the foreclosure. And to give Dusty Wilson a bit more time to see if he could rally John Barrett's friends into paying what he owed. Once she returned to Denver she would have no reason to see Dusty again.

The silence dragged on until Dusty reached out and snapped on the radio. Country music filled the cab. Deb shifted restlessly and turned her head slightly to the side, so she could see him from the corner of her eye. The words of the song blaring through the speakers were a list of things a man had to do to belong to that woman. Deb wondered what it would be like to have such a deep relationship with a man that she felt he belonged to her, and that she belonged to him.

Would Dusty meet the singer's expectations? He liked promptness. What else did he like? Probably soft and sweet and eager to do his bidding. He'd call his woman "sweetheart" or "sweetcakes" and keep her happy with those sexy smiles, with hot kisses and steamy caresses in the darkness. Or maybe not even in the dark. Weren't barns notorious for rolling in the hay?

Butterflies skittered in her stomach, her hands clenched and she swiveled her head around until she could no longer see him. At the moment she had difficulty remembering she was a businesswoman first and foremost. She was on a business trip, albeit a bit different than her normal ones. Fantasizing about the man next to her had no place here. When she attained her professional goals, she'd start looking for Mr. Right. But it wouldn't be a sexy cowboy who lived two hours from Denver!

Dusty glanced over at his passenger. She hadn't spoken a word in almost half an hour. Marjory had not been able to keep her mouth shut. Sometime he thought the silence at home was the best thing about Marjory's leaving. But he wouldn't mind Deb Harrington talking just a bit more. He'd turned on the radio to fill the silence, but maybe he should have left it off and let her fill it.

Time enough over the weekend to talk. He would take her home tonight, call John and let him know he was bringing D. Harrington tomorrow. He wanted the old man rested and in fighting form before he brought the hard-hearted banker.

Slowly he let his eyes slide over her again. She gazed out the side window, lost in thought. With her attention diverted, he could look his fill at her sexy little body. She looked like every cowboy's dream—long blond hair, pretty face, and a figure that cried out for a man's touch. He'd like to caress a breast, feel its weight, test its softness. Trace the curve of her hip and pull her up against him to feel all that softness against his own body.

From her flashes of temper, he knew she could be sparked into passion. Could a man channel that passion in bed? He'd love to try.

Whoa, the last thing this lady would do is hop into his bed. She was too focused on getting ahead to even slow down long enough to see if there were any roses, much less to stop to smell them. Of course he could try something like threats to her job. He smiled. She'd most likely knock his head off if he tried something like that. And he didn't want a woman in his bed who had to be coerced into it. He wanted her hot and ready and willing.

It had been a long time since he'd had a woman. His work took up most of his time. And there was the danger he'd get involved again, let his hormones rule, and end up married. That was a state he vowed he wouldn't enter into again.

But a fling, an affair, that could be something different. He was not a bit averse to something like that, and suspected Miss Prim and Proper Banker might like the no-ties aspect. If he could sidetrack her long enough for her to even see him as a man. Right now he knew he was the messenger, and her attention focused on the coming meeting with John. Of course, being so focused on one thing left a person vulnerable to being blindsided.

Slowly, Dusty smiled. That meeting was over twelve hours away. A lot could happen in that time.

When the ranch came into view, Dusty felt the quiet pride he always experienced over his ranch. He'd worked hard to make it in an industry that fluctuated wildly from year to year. Not only was he subject to the vagrancies of the beef market, he had capricious nature to deal with. Two winters ago when the weather had been fierce, he'd lost a large percentage of his herd. Yet he was almost back in the black—this year had been bountiful. He glanced at Deb and wondered if she found the same satisfaction with her job. How could she? Her only triumphs would be stepping on other people. Even the approaching Christmas season didn't seem to slow her down.

For a moment he forgot his interest in her as a woman and

remembered the worry she'd caused his friend. As jobs went, hers was the pits.

He turned onto the ranch road. "Welcome to the Wilson Ranch."

"That's it? Wilson Ranch?" she asked, surprised into turning to look at him.

"What did you expect?" he asked. The road wound between parallel barbed-wire fences. Cattle grazed in the field to the left. Grass rippled and danced in the wind in the field to the right.

"I don't know, maybe the Lazy W, or the Dusty Hills or something."

"My brand is the running *W,* if that helps." His lips twitched. She looked so disappointed. For a moment he considered making up a name, just to see her smile.

"You brand your cattle?"

"Of course, brand and notch. This is a cattle ranch."

"Oh." She peered over him toward the grazing cattle, as if trying to see a brand.

Dusty swung the truck over and pulled up near the fence where two steers cropped the grass, the headlights illuminating the cattle. He pulled to a stop. "See on the hip, the running *W.*"

Deb leaned closer to the windshield and studied the first cow, then she looked at the other one. They drifted to the left and she leaned over to keep them in sight until they moved out of the light, and she felt Dusty's warm breath caress her cheek. Startled, she looked up, right into blazing blue eyes. His face was inches from hers, his shoulder scant millimeters from her breasts. Knowing she should sit back in her place, Deb froze. She couldn't move, couldn't take her eyes from his as her heart rolled in her chest and began to pound.

Dusty moved his hand slowly, as if not to spook a skittish horse, and tugged on her braid. "Take this out and let your hair blow free," he said in a low, sultry voice.

As if mesmerized, Deb continued to stare into his eyes. "It's neat this way."

"It's businesslike, you mean."

She closed her eyes and slowly sank back to her place, letting the seductive tone of his voice seep through her, warming every inch of her. How did he do that? He hadn't touched her, except for her hair, yet she felt him all over. She opened her eyes and found him watching her.

Licking dry lips, she almost jumped when his eyes tracked her tongue then flicked back to her eyes.

Without another word, Dusty reached up and pulled off the ribbon then rubber band holding the braid. Slowly he worked his fingers through the hair, loosening the plait until he could comb his fingers through the shimmering waves of soft blondness.

"This isn't very businesslike," she said, wondering if her heart would burst out of her chest. She should put a stop to this immediately.

"This isn't business." That sultry tone again.

"The visit is business," she protested, trying to gather her wits about her when truly all she wanted to do was fling herself into his arms and find out how his kisses tasted.

"No, it's an exploration." He threaded his fingers through the wavy mass and pulled her face close to his. "You're on an exploration to see how John runs his ranch, and to learn more about ranches in Colorado."

"Am I on an exploration for other things, too?" she asked breathlessly, her gaze dropping to his lips.

"Maybe." With that he closed the distance between them and covered her lips with his.

Deb was startled at the instant pleasure. She liked the way his lips moved over hers, warm and firm. She liked the fluttery feelings that spread through her. His scent filled her nostrils, his taste filled her mouth when he gently thrust his tongue between her soft lips. His touch was gentle, caressing. It surprised her; she would have expected less finesse from such a virile cowboy. Would have expected hot and harsh and demanding. Instead she reveled in the sensations that lapped through her.

He deepened the kiss and she moaned softly in the back of her throat as the pleasure increased. Heat built as conscious awareness of her surroundings faded. There was only Dusty holding her, kissing her, causing the most extraordinary sensations to pulse through her.

His tongue traced her lips, licked them, slipped back inside her mouth. He bit down gently on her lower lip, then soothed it over and over with his tongue, each stroke sending tingling shafts of shimmering awareness through her body. Her breasts filled and yearned for his touch. She couldn't sit still, and squirmed slightly in the confines of the seat belt, yearning for more. Delighting in the waves of honey-sweet excitement that ebbed and flowed.

Reaching out blindly, her hand touched his throat and slid around to the back of his neck. Holding on, pulling him closer, she opened her mouth wider and let her tongue dance with his, daring to follow his into his mouth. The stunning sensations built faster and faster and she bemoaned the fact she was held in place by her seat belt. Yet she couldn't find the fastening as she clung to Dusty.

Her other hand rested on his shoulder, her fingers flexing against the hard muscle. Dimly she remembered she had wanted to touch him from the first, and now she knew how he felt. Hot, hard, and hungry. The knowledge whet her appetite for more. She tugged on his shirt, wanting to touch his bare skin. Wanting to feel that skin against her. Wanting—

"Easy, honey." Dusty backed off a couple of inches, his eyes glowing in the faint light as he gazed down at her. Satisfaction filled him. Her lips were swollen and wet from his kisses. He groaned and dropped another light kiss on her sweet lips. Did she have any idea how tempting she looked? Her cheeks shone rosy with heat, making her violet eyes shimmer almost silvery in the dim dashboard light. He rubbed one cheek with his thumb, his fingers reluctant to leave the silky softness of her hair. He could feel her breath brush across his mouth, his cheeks. She was breathing hard, as hard as he. He still wanted her. Dammit, he wanted her like he hadn't wanted a woman in a long time. If ever.

Satisfied he could find the passion he thought she contained, he could afford to take it a bit slower. If they didn't slow soon, they'd burn up right here in the truck on the main road to the ranch. They had the entire weekend ahead of them. No sense rushing things out here in the middle of nowhere. He wanted her in his bed, with no chance of interruptions. He'd leave the lights on in the bedroom so he could watch her, see every tantalizing inch of her as he made love to her until they were both too tired to move. Tonight, after the men hit the hay—

"Oh, God." Deb pulled herself out of his embrace, pushing him away, fisting her hands and staring down at them. Horror rose. What had she done? She never let herself go like that. Glancing at her watch, she saw it was scarcely eight o'clock. She'd only known the man for thirty hours! Not nearly long enough to share a kiss. And they'd shared more than one kiss. God, she thought she'd burn up. His touch was as potent as a keg of hot brandy. And she had responded like—

"You okay?"

She looked at him, at the lopsided grin, at the fire still blazing in his eyes, at the lips that had wreaked havoc on her central nervous system. She moistened her lips to reply, and tasted him again.

"I don't do things like this," she said, stunned at her response.

"Right." His smiled widened.

"I don't even know you."

"You know me better than a few minutes ago."

"I think you better take me home."

"My thoughts exactly."

Dusty put the truck in gear and accelerated up the road toward the ranch house.

"Can't you turn around on the road?"

"Home is straight ahead," he replied.

"Whose home?" she asked suspiciously.

"Mine."

"Wait a minute. What about John Barrett? I thought I was going to his ranch." A touch of panic coursed through her. Had she been set up?

"You are. First thing tomorrow morning. You need some time to look around. Then we'll talk to John in the afternoon."

"Tomorrow *afternoon?* Stop!" She reached out and caught his arm. He let go of the steering wheel with that hand and continued to drive.

"Dusty, stop this instant!"

Obligingly he slowed to a stop, then looked at her.

"What's going on?" Deb asked, her eyes dangerously narrowed as she warily watched him. Her emotions were on overload. If she didn't get some straight answers soon, she'd explode.

"Do you need to take notes, so you can refer to them if things get out of hand?" Dusty asked dryly.

"Talk, cowboy, and it better be something I want to hear."

"Or what, you'll get out and walk home in a huff?"

She glanced out the back window. The road to the highway was dark and empty. She'd find no help around here.

"I don't know what's going on." Suddenly the vulnerability of her position hit her. She liked working at the bank because she knew exactly what to do and expect. This situation confused her, left her totally unsure of anything.

He relented. "We'll see John tomorrow. I'll show you around his ranch before we meet him. That way you'll see everything before talking to him, and he won't get tired trying to convince you about the stability of his spread. He's sick. I told you that. He's recovering, but slowly. I don't want him worn out seeing you."

"I thought I was staying at his place."

"It's nearby. I have things to do here. We'll go over tomorrow."

She wanted to ask about the kiss, but couldn't form the words. Silently she stared at him, almost willing him to respond to her unasked questions.

He reached out, brushed her lips with a fingertip, and rubbed the back of his fingers against her cheek. "Are you still as pink as the roses my mother grows?"

Swallowing hard, Deb took a breath.

"No, don't say it." He shook his head. "There's an attraction between us. I can't be the only one to feel it."

"I came on business."

"And where is it written that you can't combine business with pleasure?"

"And where is it written that a woman must submit to a man just because—"

"Hold on, honey. You gave as good as you got in those kisses."

Deb opened her mouth, then promptly closed it. He was right, on all counts. She was attracted, much more than she should be. And she had responded. And he was the last man in the world she wanted to fall for.

"Then I apologize."

"Why, didn't you like it?"

She looked out the windshield, afraid to let him see her face, afraid he'd see how much she had enjoyed it. But no more. Her plans didn't include a cowboy.

"Deb?"

"Yes, all right, I liked it. But that's all. I'm here on business, not for your entertainment."

"I don't know, you seem to be doing all right so far." His sharp reply caused her to look at him again. Anger seemed to simmer just below the surface.

"I don't go in for casual sex, so if you think that's where we'll end up this weekend, disabuse yourself of that notion immediately!"

"Are those big banker words? Words a vice president uses?"

"I'm not a vice president."

"Yet. Isn't that what comes next? Isn't that why you're here, to smooth this situation over so nothing interferes with moving up the ladder?"

"I see you got more than my address from my secretary."

"Yeah. Foolish girl admires you. Wants to be just like you. Except she'll never make it. She's too warm and friendly and likable."

Deb schooled her features. She would not let him know how

the barb had hurt. She had heard it before, it shouldn't matter anymore.

Clearing her throat, she turned away, wishing she could beam herself somewhere else and never have to lay eyes on this disturbing man again.

''I would like to go home. My home,'' she said.

''Tough, we're here and you're staying until you've seen John.''

Three

Dusty pulled up near a two-story clapboard house. The sun had set hours ago behind the western hills that sheltered the valley. Soft lamplight fell through the sparkling front window on the left. Deb peered out, trying to see everything. She had never been on a ranch before. Vaguely in the light from the moon she could make out the outline of a half dozen buildings, some with lights showing, others in total darkness. She wished she knew what purpose each one served.

"We missed dinner, but I think Ivy will feed us," Dusty said as he shut off the engine.

"We could have stopped somewhere on the drive in," she commented, opening her door. The air was crisp and cold, redolent with unfamiliar fragrances—fresh pine, dust, horse and cattle. It wasn't unpleasant. She took a second breath and turned toward the house, following Dusty.

"Not much on manners," she muttered as she mounted the steps still reeling from their kiss. She had to find something to put a distance between them.

"Thought you businesswomen wanted equality," he

drawled as he held the door open. "You can't have it both ways, sweetcakes." He'd taken her case from the truck bed and set it just inside the door.

Deb opened her mouth to respond but never got a word in. His finger covered her lips.

"Don't argue now. I'll see about some grub. You can take any of the rooms upstairs except mine." He grinned down at her, his finger moving to her cheek. "On second thought, you can take any room upstairs that you please."

The brief brush against her skin seemed to brand her. Her breath caught and she trembled slightly.

She jerked away. "In your dreams."

"Maybe. I'll be right back."

Before she could ask where he was going, he'd disappeared into the darkness. She moved to the door and watched him cross to a long, low building several yards away. Lights blazed from windows, a rectangle of light appeared as he opened the door. Then he disappeared inside. Nothing stirred in the quiet evening. The breeze was light, blowing from the hills, cold and tangy and heavy laden with pine scent.

She closed the door and picked up her case, heading for the stairs at the back of the hallway. On the way she peeped into the rooms she passed. On her left was a large, comfortable living room. A television stood in the corner, an elaborate stereo against one wall. Centered on the opposite wall, the fireplace was cavernous. Dusty probably needed every bit of heat he could get in the winter. A comfortable sofa sat before it, covered in a tweedy fabric of blues and browns and whites. The coffee table had scars she'd bet anything came from Dusty resting his feet on it while watching television.

To the right was a dining room. The drapes were closed, the table empty. Two more doors lined the hall, but both were closed. Deb didn't open them. She climbed the wooden stairs, her soft running shoes making scarcely a sound. Dusty's hard-soled boots would announce his arrival.

The first room she saw was his. For a long moment she stood at the doorway and gazed in at the masculine decor. A huge bed dominated the center. He could sleep in it with five other people and still not get crowded, she thought. The dark blue coverlet drooped to the floor. White curtains outlined the windows in a manner that wouldn't interfere with any view. All the furniture appeared polished and well cared for. Did Dusty do the housework? She couldn't picture it.

She turned reluctantly and headed down the hall, to the farthest door on the right. Opening it, she found an elegantly furnished room, with sleek modern furniture and lamps. The distance from his room suited Deb.

Searching behind the other hallway doors led her to the bathroom. A quick wash, her hair tidied, and she felt better. It had been a long day, a long drive out, and she was tired. She would have liked to forget dinner, but she hadn't eaten any lunch and was starving.

"Deb?" Dusty called.

"Coming." Hurrying down the stairs, she looked into the dining room. He had flipped on the light, placed two plates side by side and tossed down a handful of utensils.

"Ivy kept it warm for us. Dig in." He stood behind a chair, waited for her, then seated her like the very best of waiters.

"Ivy is the cook, I take it," she said as she pulled one plate closer. The stew looked heavenly, smelled even better. There were two huge slabs of cornbread dripping with melting butter. Her mouth watered as she reached for a fork.

"Right. She's married to Hank, one of my best hands. She cooks for the whole crew."

"Are most of your cowboys married?"

"No, only Hank, Steve and Bart. The rest are too smart."

Deb ignored the comment, intent on the delicious food before her. She ate quietly, daintily, but as fast as she dared. She couldn't remember when anything had tasted so good.

"If Ivy does the cooking around here, what do the other wives do?" she asked when the silence threatened to drag on forever. Dusty was a man of few words.

"Susan and Steve are newlyweds. She works in town at the local hardware store. Jessie's the receptionist for Doc Harvey, also in town. She and Susan ride in together now that Susan lives here."

"And they all live where?"

"All but Ivy and Hank live in the bunkhouse. They have a small cottage on the rim. I think Bart and Jessie want a place of their own, and are saving up for it. Steve and Susan don't care where they are, as long as they have privacy."

"I take it the bunkhouse isn't like in the old cowboy movies where everyone has a bed against the wall." Deb broke off another bit of cornbread, popped it into her mouth. She ought to get the recipe from this Ivy, it was melt-in-her-mouth delicious.

He smiled slowly, and her heart kicked over. She looked back at her plate. It was much safer than letting herself go to mush because of that lopsided smile that drove her crazy!

"No, it's not like that."

"How many people work on the ranch?" She turned the subject, not wanting to delve into newlyweds' love lives, or how they lived.

"I have eight men, Ivy, and some high school kids who help out when we need them," he replied.

"And Mr. Barrett, how many men work on his place?"

"Five, last I heard. Lester is his foreman, and has been keeping the place going since John's been sick."

"What's he sick from?" She'd been curious about that since Dusty barged into her office yesterday. Was it only yesterday?

"Had bronchitis that went into pneumonia. Then he got a staph infection that almost did him in."

"He'll be all right?"

"Yeah, he's well on the road to recovery. But he lost a lot of weight, and he's not a young man. It'll be a while yet before he's completely recovered."

She nodded. She'd dealt with the loan application, she'd read all the pertinent information. John Barrett was sixty-two. While not young, he still had a lot of years before him, if he could get well.

"How far is his ranch from here?" she asked, remembering why she was there.

"His spread joins this one on the north side. We'll ride over tomorrow and you can see what he's got. Then we'll stop in and see him. That suit you?"

"What time tomorrow?"

Dusty slowly smiled, his eyes sparkling. "Didn't we say six-thirty? How early do you want to get up?"

Deb watched him warily. She didn't trust his smile. Didn't trust him an inch. Or was it herself she didn't trust around him? God, six-thirty was early.

"We'll eat with the men at seven, then get the horses—"

"Horses!"

He put down his fork. "What did you think we'd ride, bulls?"

"I thought you meant the truck. I can't ride a horse."

"Why not?"

"I never have. I didn't come here to go riding on some horse."

"We'll just walk, you won't fall off. Best way to get a firsthand look at John's spread. We'll go where a truck couldn't."

"I prefer a truck, or even a car," she said primly. The thought of getting on a horse shook her. She'd never even been close to one. "I certainly don't need to ride a horse."

"That's why you came—isn't it?—to see John's place and talk to him. Well, the best way to see it is on the back of a horse." He balled up his napkin and tossed it on the table. Shoving back his chair, he rose and leaned over toward Deb, the flash of anger showing in his eyes, in the sharp edge of his voice. "Or maybe you have another way to accomplish all that? Maybe hire a helicopter and get a bird's-eye view of the ranch? I'm sure your rich bank could manage that just fine. Or forget trying to work out a compromise and just foreclose! That's what you've wanted all along."

He straightened. "I was a fool to think this weekend would change your attitude. We're riding, make up your mind to it! And you better go with an open mind. If you don't give serious consideration to holding off on that foreclosure, I can still talk to Montgomery!" Dusty practically yelled the last sentence.

"I don't—" She shut her mouth and stared at her plate as she heard the stomp of boots as Dusty swiftly crossed the room and headed down the hall. The old fear bubbled to the surface. She took a deep breath, trying to push it down. She hated confrontations. She hated yelling voices and angry stances. She just wanted to hide inside herself until everything was calm again. Hide away from trouble and make sure it didn't find her. Since being on her own, she swore she wouldn't ever get in such a situation again.

Slowly she placed her fork on the almost-empty plate. She was thirsty, the meal had been delicious, but Dusty brought no beverage. Taking another deep breath, she could feel her nerves begin to calm. Rising, she headed for the door in the back. Pushing through, she found the kitchen. Deb considered giving up and returning home as she searched for a glass. Surely she could get someone on the ranch to take her to the nearest town, and then she could find some sort of transportation. It was obvious she wouldn't last the weekend with Dusty Wilson.

She'd have to speak to Mr. Montgomery first thing Monday, to attempt to defuse anything Dusty would say.

Dusty stomped into his office, leaving the door open for fear he'd slam it if he closed it. He crossed to the window and leaned his arm against the frame, his forehead resting against it. Damnation! He didn't know if he was more angry with himself or John for putting him in this mess. He'd practically dragged this city woman to the ranch and then berated her just because she hesitated about riding.

And the worst part was, his anger had nothing to do with riding, or John. It had to do with the ache riding him down low, with the desire that couldn't be curbed. He wanted her. Watching her eat had been a turn-on. Hell, watching her breathe was a turn-on. She had brushed her hair since they arrived, but left it down. How was a man supposed to eat when he wanted to wrap those silky strands around his fist and draw her mouth to his? How could a man concentrate on anything when she licked the gravy from the corner of her lip and he fantasized about her licking his lips? When her mouth bit into warm corn bread, and he wished she was nibbling on him?

Yet the first time he suggested something out of the proper venue for a staid banker, she'd balked. She could enjoy riding. And they'd see a lot more of John's spread if they rode.

But she was here under protest, because he'd convinced her to give the man another look before foreclosing. Maybe she was just going through the motions, maybe she had no intention of stalling the foreclosure.

That didn't make sense. Deb Harrington was obviously not enjoying herself. She was ill at ease, and uncertain. Why come, if she didn't intend to seriously think about reversing her decision? For all her determination to get ahead, he sensed a strong sense of integrity in the woman. She was trying.

Now he'd made a mess of that by yelling at her. She'd looked half frightened. But she had to know he was all bark and no bite. Well, for the most part. Unless he got really riled. He shook his head. He hadn't gotten really riled in a long time. Which was a good thing as anyone who knew him could attest.

Grimly he smiled. He'd forgo the barking part if he could do a bit of biting. But only if she didn't fear him. They would be between the sheets on his bed and nibbling would give her more pleasure than— With a groan, he moved away from the window and went to sit behind the desk. He had more important things to do than fantasize about some fast-track female executive out to reach the top of the heap.

Business. The lady was only here on business. Once she saw John, she'd demand to be taken home and that would be that. He'd probably never see her again. And that was for the best. He didn't want to get tangled up with some dedicated, dyed-in-the-wool businesswoman with her eye on the main chance. He'd played that game once before. It wasn't for him. So she could keep her sexy little body covered up in dull suits, keep that glorious hair confined to boring French braids and spend her money on fancy condos and foreign cars. He didn't need her.

Of course, *want* was a different issue.

He heard her steps on the stairs. Hesitating only a moment, he rose and followed her upstairs. Dusty instinctively knew which room she'd taken, the farthest from his. He walked down the hall and knocked on the door.

"Yes?" Deb opened it, her eyes wary, watchful.

"Towels and things are in the cupboard in the bathroom. Help yourself."

She nodded and started to close the door.

His hand held it open. "Do you need me to wake you up tomorrow?"

"If you would." She pushed, he didn't budge.

"We never decided on a time."

"I thought we were eating with your men at seven. I guess I need to get up by six-thirty to be ready."

"I'll knock."

Deb pushed again and slowly he dropped his hand. When the door was shut, Dusty waited until he heard her footsteps moving away from the door before he turned to head back downstairs. So much for continuing what they'd started in the car. She had erected a wall too thick to pierce tonight. Maybe tomorrow. If his temper didn't flare again.

"Dusty, wondered when you'd wander in this morning." A tall, dark woman stood near a huge stove in the bunkhouse kitchen and grinned at him as he escorted Deb inside the next morning.

"This your new lady friend?" one of the men drawled.

Chuckles drew Deb's gaze as she looked around the huge country kitchen. Gleaming industrial-size equipment lined one wall. A huge table with chairs along both sides filled the center of the room. Cupboards and counters extended along two more walls. There were half a dozen or more people seated around the long pine table and beyond was a bank of wide windows that offered a view that didn't quit. Coffee brewed on the stove, the fragrance of bacon and biscuits already filled the room.

"Ivy, want you to meet Deborah Harrington." Dusty tossed his hat to the left, making sure it landed on the rack mounted

on the wall before turning back to take Deb's jacket from her.
He hung both jackets on the rack below his hat.

"Deb, this wonderful woman is Ivy Waters, chief cook and
bottle washer for the ranch. Deb liked your stew last night,
Ivy. Appreciate your keeping something warm for us. We
couldn't leave Denver any earlier yesterday. Deb works at the
bank."

At that, everything stopped, every eye in the room focused
on Deb.

She swallowed and tried a smile. There wasn't a friendly
face in the crowd. Bewildered, she glanced at Dusty.

He sauntered across the room, so sure of himself. She hesitated, unsure where she should sit, or even if she should stay
in light of the sudden hostile silence.

"When will breakfast be ready? My stomach thinks my
throat's been cut," Dusty asked, pulling out a chair.

Ivy whacked him in the stomach with the back of her hand.
"You could stand to go without a meal or two. Putting on a
bit, aren't you?"

Deb's gaze dropped to that tight stomach. The man didn't
have a spare ounce of flesh on him, she knew that for certain.
Heat curled through her as she remembered being pressed
against him last night, her fingers tingled at the remembered
feel of his muscles.

"Ah, maybe I could, but we want to show off our hospitality to the banker, now don't we?"

Ivy looked around Dusty, her eyes scanning Deb from head
to toe. She shrugged. "Have a seat, and I'll get your breakfast,
hon," she said, ignoring Dusty.

"Ivy, you need any help?" the woman seated on the right
asked, her eyes watching Deb. She was young, looked about
twenty, with short blond hair and a tan that made her hair
seem even lighter.

"Now, Susie, I can handle one more for breakfast, and even
if I couldn't, Dusty could just eat less and share his meal with
half the rest of you."

The chuckles eased some of the tension in the room. Dusty
motioned for Deb to sit. He leaned close and whispered in her

ear, "Hope those jeans stretch a bit. Ivy's cooking is the best there is and you need a big breakfast to hold you today."

She knew by the satisfied look in his eye that color had flashed into her cheeks at his audacious comment. Wisely, she refrained from replying. What could she say with almost a dozen people straining to hear every word?

Windows brought the outdoors almost inside and her place at the table enabled her to see the mountains. That is, once she could see anything beyond the shimmering haze that clouded her vision when Dusty's breath skimmed her cheek, when his hand brushed against her arm, deliberately. There was a dusting of snow on the distant peaks, but none on the ground near the ranch. It had been a dry fall, and warmer than usual. She wondered how the hills would look covered in snow.

Dusty sat across from her, his amused eyes challenging her.

He knew the effect he had on her, she thought, fuming. Time to show Mr. Wilson she didn't care a snap about him or his audacious teasing.

"Listen up, Deb, and see how good your memory is," he said, then promptly began to name each person seated at the table. By the time he'd reached the last man, Deb knew she was in trouble. She couldn't remember all the names, much less which one belonged to whom. And with her luck, Dusty would ask her to repeat them all. At least she knew the women, Jessie, Susan and Ivy.

"So you're the banker foreclosing on old John," Ivy said as she plopped a plate in front of Deb.

"Actually, that's why I'm here, to reconsider the situation," Deb responded, amazed the eggs had not slid off.

"Should have done that before telling John you were taking his place. Didn't sit well with the folks around here," Ivy said, handing out more plates. The cowboys seemed used to her handling the food and appeared unconcerned as eggs slithered dangerously close to the edges of all the plates as Ivy plopped each one on the table.

Deb was torn between defending herself and keeping quiet about bank business. It wasn't anyone's concern. And she didn't know these people. Yet she wanted them to understand she had not wanted to foreclose, but it had been necessary. If she were to progress in the bank, the top people had to know she could be depended upon to do all aspects of her job, not just the easy or pleasant ones.

"Now, Ivy, don't jump all over Deb. She was just doing her job. Right, sweetcakes? She's a by-the-book kind of gal. We should be grateful she's decided to check things out on her own. She just might reverse the decision."

Deb glared at him. If he called her "sweetcakes" again, she was liable to scream, or dump her eggs on him.

"John Barrett runs a good spread. He's good for the money," one of the cowhands said.

"Anyway some of us are taking up a collection to tide him over. Your bank will get its money," Susan said. "We've even got folks from town contributing. It's not much now, but the account is growing every day."

"I think that's admirable—"

"Hell, John's a friend. We stick by friends out here," another cowboy said.

Deb looked around the table wistfully. This was the second time she'd heard that mentioned. It pointed out the dearth in her own life of close friends, of people who would go to such lengths for her sake.

"We'll be heading out soon, so eat up," Dusty said. "Josh, when you're done, saddle up Starlight for me, would you?"

"Sure, boss, want Diego, too?"

"I can saddle my own horse," Dusty growled as he took a healthy swig of hot coffee.

Josh grinned and nodded.

"You two riding over to John's?" Ivy asked, finally seating herself beside a tall, thin man. She nudged him to pass the butter, then turned her attention back to Dusty.

"Yeah. Thought Deb should see some of what John's done. Make sure she knows he's good for the money."

"Do much riding in Denver, hon?" Ivy asked.

Deb shook her head, about to admit to never having ridden before, but Dusty spoke first.

"Starlight will carry her just fine. We won't be home for lunch, but will do our best to work up an appetite for dinner."

"Huh? Your breathing works up an appetite. Take some apples or something to tide you over. Deb doesn't look like she'll last all day without food."

Deb smiled at Ivy. "I often go without lunch when I'm caught up in something at work. I'll be fine, thanks."

Dusty's good mood vanished. "What's eating compared to getting ahead, right, Deb?"

She ignored his remark and ate her breakfast. Gradually the others began talking about the work ahead. Susan and the small dark-haired woman called Jessie finished first. Both kissed the men beside them, then cleared their places, stacking the dishes and cups in the sink. Waving a cheery goodbye, they left. In only moments the sound of their car was heard driving away.

Deb listened with interest as the men discussed water holes and fencing repairs. She was totally lost when one of them began talking about some problem with a cow and questioning if they should bring in the vet. Dusty vetoed the vet, recommending a course of treatment as a first round. When she finished eating, Ivy refilled her coffee cup and whisked away her plate.

"I could clear it for you," Deb said, surprised by the move.

"You're a guest, hon, no problem."

"Going to take mine?" Dusty asked, leaning back in his chair, tilting it on two legs.

"Not in this lifetime, cowboy. You know the rules," Ivy said gruffly. She met Deb's startled glance and winked.

The men began to move. Each picked up his plate and cup and marched by the sink on the way out until only Ivy, Dusty and Deb remained.

"Can I help with dishes?" Deb asked in a shy voice. She wasn't sure of the protocol here; if even the boss had to bus his own table, who was she to be waited on?

"You'll have enough to do if you're going riding with the Lone Ranger here. I've been managing these dishes for close to seven years. I reckon I can manage this morning. Thanks anyway, hon.''

''Ready to ride?'' Dusty asked, bringing his chair down with a bang. He scooped up his plate and deposited it in the sink. ''Good breakfast, Ivy, thanks.''

Deb rose and headed for the door. If she hadn't needed her jacket, she would have reached the door before him, get outside and put some distance between them. But it was too cold to forget her jacket.

He lengthened his stride, snatched his hat from the rack and then snagged both jackets. Tossing his over his shoulder, he held Deb's for her. She hesitated, then donned it with his help. When his fingers deliberately brushed against her neck, pulling her hair from beneath her jacket, she shivered. Had they been alone, would he have spun her around and kissed her?

She pulled away. Dusty opened the door. Leaning across the opening, he halfway blocked it, forcing her to brush past him to get outside. His tantalizing aftershave tickled her nostrils. She took a breath and smelled the scent of horses and hay and sexy cowboy. It started a slow throb deep inside, which only added to her wish for another kiss. How was she going to get through this day if she spent it fantasizing about this man?

Disturbed, she stepped outside. She never felt like this about men. She went months at a time without a single date. She could not get some fixation on a cowboy. And especially not this cowboy!

When she reached the dirt in the yard, she headed quickly for the huge barn.

''Where's the fire, sweetcakes?'' Dusty fell into step beside her, shrugging on his jacket.

''Don't call me that!'' she said, looking straight ahead.

''You'll need a hat. The sun's brutal at this elevation, even in winter. Don't want to get burned for Christmas. We'll find you one in the barn.''

''If we took the truck, I wouldn't have to worry about a hat.''

''Scared?'' he taunted.

She shook her head. Maybe she was just a little, but she'd die before letting him know. The closer she came to the horse tied to the fence, the bigger he looked. The stirrup hung several feet above the ground. How would she ever get her foot into one and haul herself up on the beast? And once there, could she stick?

"Starlight's an old horse. She'll give you an easy ride. The good thing is, she doesn't want to run any more than you want her to," Dusty said in a gentle voice.

"I don't know about this, Dusty," Deb replied, eyeing the horse warily.

"I wouldn't let anything happen to you," he said, turning her around to face him. "Not until you reverse the foreclosure on John's property."

The bubble of joy that had begun to grow burst with the final sentence. Afraid her disappointment might show, she dropped her gaze to his throat. She knew he didn't like her, so why did his comment hurt? He'd been teasing, there was no malice.

"Come on, meet Starlight." Dusty took her arm and led her to the old mare. "She's a nice old girl."

"I thought it was a boy horse."

He chuckled, she looked very serious. Somehow his teasing hadn't gotten the rise out of her he'd expected. In fact, he almost thought he'd hurt her feelings. Impossible, he knew. Hard-hearted businesswomen were impervious to hurt feelings. They stepped on others on their way to the top, mindless of any casualties they left behind.

"Dusty, I can't ride this horse. She's huge." Deb could scarcely look over the back of the saddle. The stirrups were about waist level. She couldn't even get on the darn thing.

"Sure you can." Without another word, he put his hands on her waist and lifted. "Swing your right leg over the saddle."

In seconds she was seated on the warm leather, looking down a long way to the man grinning beside her.

"See, you're on. When we start riding, just sit in the saddle and guide her with the reins." He drew the reins from the horse's neck and wrapped the fingers of her right hand around the single line. "She's neck-reined trained. Push your hand that way to turn left, this way to go right. Got it?"

Half scared, half exultant, Deb nodded. Dusty beckoned her closer. Balancing precariously, she leaned closer until she could see the faint lines radiating from his eyes, until she could see the sparkle and teasing lights.

"What?"

"This." His hand reached behind her head and drew her down until his lips touched hers. "A kiss for luck," he murmured against her mouth, releasing her slowly.

Deb gripped the horn of the saddle, afraid she'd slide right off. Her heart pounded and blood rushed through her veins. Heat engulfed her again. Damn the man, he was driving her insane.

"Luck, huh? You'd better watch it, cowboy, 'cause you're the one needing luck," she said bravely, hoping he wouldn't challenge her show of bravado.

"You don't like kissing? Next time, bite my lip and I'll stop." He gently slapped her thigh before walking around her horse and heading inside the barn.

"Now what?" Deb called, afraid to move a muscle lest it startle the horse. Her leg felt the imprint of his hand. For a moment she wanted him to come back, touch her again. Maybe even offer another kiss for luck. It beat being stuck on a strange horse all by herself.

"I'm getting Diego, I'll be out in a couple of minutes. Want me to untie Starlight?"

"No, we'll wait right here until you're ready."

Gingerly Deb patted the horse, her mind spinning. *Next time,* he'd said. He planned to kiss her again? She would have to be more forceful in protesting. Tell him she didn't want any kisses, no caresses. She was there on business!

Though he didn't seem to be impressed. In fact he was downright scathing about her career ambitions. She wished she knew more about his wife, what she'd been like, how she'd hurt him. Maybe she could act a bit differently, to minimize any comparison with Marjory. Did the woman regret the divorce? Deb knew if she ever married, she would want a loving, lasting relationship. She wouldn't take such vows lightly.

But there was the possibility she'd never marry. She couldn't forget what her mother had endured with her father. How could anyone know what the future held? Would she ever be brave enough to risk it? Her life was satisfying now. She had her career, a nice place to live, her car. Maybe when she made V.P. she'd change, or maybe she'd work her way up straight to the top, becoming the first woman president of the bank.

"Yo, Deb. Here." Dusty rode out of the barn and tossed a hat toward her. She caught it, and gingerly placed it on her head. Instantly her eyes were shaded. It cut the sun's glare dramatically.

"Thanks. Now I feel like a real cowboy," she mumbled, feeling more like a scared city girl than ever.

"A real cowboy wears boots, we'll have to get you some."

"I'll pass. Who unties the horse?"

He rode up beside her, crowding against Starlight until the mare moved almost parallel to the fence. Leaning out from his saddle, he unfastened the lead line from the bridle and let it hang from the top rail.

"Let's ride."

"Right." She took a deep breath. Would Mr. Montgomery at the bank appreciate all she was doing to make sure this account didn't end up a bad debt? Probably not. Now if Phil Moore was doing this, Montgomery would probably give him an extra day off or a raise. But she couldn't dwell on the probable actions of her co-workers. She had to concentrate on riding.

To her surprise, Deb enjoyed herself. The mare followed Dusty's gelding with no prompting, moving easily right or left as Deb instructed with the reins. Gradually Deb relaxed and began to take stock of her surroundings.

At their slow pace, it took almost a half hour to reach Barrett land. Deb didn't waste a second of it, however. She had dozens of questions for Dusty about his own place, about the cattle she saw, the fallow fields, the fencing and the water holes. She had him explain the conversations at breakfast and led the discussion into his plans for the future.

He was a good tour guide. When they reached the boundary of John's land, Dusty explained everything they saw, always painting John Barrett in a very favorable light.

"You're a wonderful advocate for the man," Deb said late in the morning. She was getting tired, longed to change her position, but she was too afraid of making any moves in case the horse didn't like it. Just how big was this spread?

"I'm only telling you the truth. He hit a bad patch, Deb. He just needs to get over it. Your bank is not going to lose out on the deal." He eyed her shifting in the seat. "Getting tired?"

"Yes. Is it much farther to his house?"

"About twenty minutes. We'll see it in a bit."

There was still the ride back to the Wilson Ranch, but she didn't care, the thought of getting off the horse for a while perked her up. She'd deal with the return trip later.

Cresting a slight rise, Deb could see the back of a large barn, a corral encircling one side. "That it?" she asked.

Dusty nodded.

Just then Starlight stumbled. Deb shrieked, clutching the saddle horn and squeezing the horse with her legs. Dancing sideways several steps, Starlight came to a halt when Dusty urged Diego up beside her and reached for the reins.

"Oh, my God, I thought I was going to fall!" Deb said, holding on to the saddle for dear life.

"What happened?" Dusty asked, easing back on the reins.

"I don't know. We were following you, then she seemed to trip. Her head went down and I almost got pulled over."

Dusty quickly dismounted and handed her his reins. Running his hands down Starlight's front legs, he lifted each hoof in turn and examined them. Standing, he shook his head. "Can't see anything wrong." He swung up into the saddle with a smooth, seemingly effortless motion.

"How long have you been riding?" Deb asked, wishing she could be as graceful.

"Since I was a kid. Come on. The sooner we get to John's, the sooner you can get off the horse."

"Not too soon for me." Two seconds later Deb called, "Dusty! She's limping."

He watched for a moment, then sighed. "You're getting off sooner than expected. Somehow she's injured that front leg. I can't let you stay on."

"It's not far to the house, I can walk that distance." Deb wasn't unhappy to be dismounting. Her legs felt like spaghetti.

Dusty swung down. Holding his reins, he came to lift her down.

"I can manage," she protested.

"Your legs will need a minute to adjust," he said. Letting her hold on to the saddle, he held her until strength flowed back into her legs.

His proximity did nothing to strengthen her knees, it was just another nail in the coffin of her good intentions to stay away from this sexy cowboy.

Four

"Sorry, there's no automobile service out here, sweetcakes," Dusty said as they started off on foot toward the house in the distance. He led the two horses, walking slowly as Starlight limped along behind him.

"Meaning?" Deb asked, stretching her legs and trying not to wince at the tight muscles.

"If you were in Denver and your fancy sports car broke, you'd find a phone and call the automobile club. Presto, instant service."

She nodded. "Actually, I have a car phone, so that would be no problem. If this kind of thing happens often, maybe you should consider a similar service," she said seriously.

Dusty chuckled and shook his head. "Everything can't be made convenient."

"What would have happened if the horse had hurt her leg half an hour ago?" Deb asked.

"You would ride with me, same as on the way home. What did you think, that I'd leave you stranded someplace?"

"Ride with you on the way home? Can't you get someone

from the ranch to come get us?'' She'd had enough riding to last a lifetime. And there was no way she would get on a horse with him. She couldn't see how they could ride double without being in very close contact. Too close for peace of mind.

"The men have their chores, the women are at work. No one has time to come get us."

"You know, Dusty, you're the boss of that ranch. If you order someone to do something, they have to do it. I think you are a bit lax with your personnel."

"Is that a fact?"

"This morning Ivy didn't clear your place. In fact, when you asked her to, her response bordered on being insubordinate. You're the boss, she should have taken yours before mine."

"Is that how it works in business?" His voice was dangerously low, his drawl deceptively easy.

"It's like the military. The higher-ups give orders to the ones below them. Chain of command makes things a lot easier. I could give you some pointers if you'd like to improve the efficiency of your staff. I've worked with staff restructuring at the bank and—'' Deb stopped when she realized Dusty had stopped. Turning, she met his gaze.

He stared hard at her, his eyes narrowed and angry. "Listen up, woman, because I'm not going to say this twice. My ranch and how I run it is off limits to you completely. I've handled things the way I want for over four years now. I don't need some hoity-toity businesswoman coming in and throwing her weight around like she's a gift from the gods with her pseudo-military structures and rigid job lines. Marjory tried the same thing, which riled me no end. One thing you miss in your frantic climb to the top is the pure joy of life. You're too busy scrambling and covering your butt to make friends and just plain enjoy life."

"That's not true! I enjoy life. I have nice clothes, a great car, a super condo that cost half the earth, and I earned every bit of it myself."

"Show-off. What other material things do you flaunt to everyone so they'll know how successful you are? And do your friends cheer you on? Or do they try to outshine you? Is the competition limited to the office, or are you in some huge race with everyone you know to see who gets the most expensive car and house?''

She blinked and took a breath. Unable to meet the heat in his gaze, she looked away, first toward the house. But the memory of why she was there pricked. She scanned the hills, wishing she could run away as fast she could and never have to see this man again.

''I worked hard to get what I have, to get where I am in my job. It's all I have and I won't let you belittle it. Maybe I can't live some lazy laid-back life like you and all your friends do, but this is my life and it's the way I want it. I'm sorry if my success somehow offends you, but if you knew what I've overcome to get here—'' She stopped abruptly and lifted her hat, gazing for a moment at the clear blue sky. Settling the hat on her head, she blinked her eyes hard. She would not give way to tears, no matter how frustrated or angry or upset he made her.

Without another word, she began walking toward the house. If she was going to meet with John Barrett, she wanted to get it over with and get back to Denver. She should never have been coerced into coming. If she had simply stated the bank's position and proceeded, none of this would be happening. This is what she got for caring about some man she'd never met. And being intrigued with a wild cowboy who stormed her office shooting threats left and right.

''Deb, wait.''

''I have a job to do, Mr. Wilson. The sooner I interview the client, the sooner I can get home.'' She didn't look around, but picked up her pace until she was almost breathless.

When Dusty's hand grabbed her arm, Deb swung around, surprised. He'd covered the ground swiftly and silently. The horses stood behind his right shoulder, watching the two of them curiously, ears pricked forward.

''Hold on a minute. You can be mad at me all you want, but don't let your anger spill over into dealing with John, you understand?''

"Or what? You'll call the local newspaper and have it blasted over the front page?"

"Whatever it takes, sweetcakes. Do we have a deal?"

"What we have is coercion. But I am professional enough to put aside my own personal feelings and do what is best for the bank."

Dusty could feel the anger begin to boil up inside. He wanted to shake her, she was so damn snooty with her profession, her image and her damned aloof manner. "I don't give a damn about your precious bank."

"If your money was in it you would want me to do the best job I could to safeguard it," she replied. "I have a fiduciary responsibility—"

He did shake her at that, slightly, just enough to stop the flow of words. "I'm not asking you to do anything against banking rules. Just give the man a fair hearing. Afterward you can rant and rave at me all you want."

"Afterward, I'm going home!" She yanked her arm free and headed for the house.

Dusty watched her go. "That's what you think, sweetcakes," he muttered. Though why he didn't just have one of the men run her home was beyond him. There was no need to have her stay the weekend. As prickly and *professional* as she was, he should be glad to get rid of her.

But watching that pert bottom sway as she made her way over the broken ground drove thoughts of leaving from his mind. Her figure was compact and trim. She curved in all the right places and the snug jeans she wore did nothing to hide her shape like her drab business suits did. In those pants, she was definitely female.

And it made him very conscious of being male. A male with a hunger for a certain blonde who he had no business even thinking about, especially in those terms. He shook his head and started to follow her. She'd probably run screaming in the opposite direction if she had a clue to his thoughts. But it didn't hurt a man to dream, and with an armful of femininity like Deb Harrington, a man could dream of dying happy.

When Deb reached the yard to the Barrett house, she was

hot, dusty, damp with perspiration and feeling totally unprofessional. She couldn't imagine trying to conduct any kind of business attired as she was. The facade of professionalism she worked so hard to acquire was nowhere evident. She glanced down at her dusty jeans and shoes. Lifting the sides of her jacket away from her body, she fanned herself for a second. Turning, she looked for Dusty. He'd gotten her this far, the least he could do was introduce her to the man she'd come to see.

She spotted him leading the horses toward the barn. Sorry that her mount had injured herself, Deb watched with sympathy as the old mare limped patiently along behind the tall cowboy.

Hesitating, Deb finally gave a sigh and headed for the barn.

"Do you want to introduce me to your friend, or shall I just go on in?" she asked once her eyes adjusted to the dimmer light and she saw Dusty in the back tying the horses to a rail.

"I'm coming, let me unsaddle Starlight. I'll ask John if I can board her here for a few days."

She watched him work. With an efficiency of motion, he took down the saddle, released the bridle and had the horse in a stall in a matter of minutes. Loosening the girth on his own saddle, he made sure Diego had water, then turned to head out to the house. Deb fell into step as he approached. Nervously she wiped her hands on her jeans.

"I should have worn a suit," she mumbled, wishing she had the accoutrements of her profession. It helped her feel more in charge of things.

"You'll do just as you are. John's not one to stand on ceremony. If you came in your banker outfit, you'd probably intimidate the hell out of him."

"Right, like I could intimidate anyone."

"Honey, I bet you intimidate any man who looks at you."

"Just because most men want fluff and frills doesn't mean there aren't some out there who appreciate brains," she retorted.

"Brains are exactly what I think of when I look at you," he drawled.

Deb didn't care that the remark hurt. She couldn't help looking the way she looked. Her clothes helped her move ahead in the bank. And she knew she accomplished what she'd done on work, not because of any patronizing tokenism. Mr. Montgomery didn't even want women in her position. He thought they were fine as tellers, without the responsibility that would take them away from being wives or mothers. Dusty obviously thought the same way, if his comments about his wife were any indication. Ex-wife.

They reached the house and Dusty walked in as if he owned the place.

"John?" he called.

"In here." The voice responding was frail.

Deb looked around, and took off the borrowed hat. Running her fingers over her hair, she hoped it didn't look too hopelessly awful.

Following Dusty into the living room, she immediately saw the elderly man sitting by the window.

"Hey, Dusty, good to see you."

"Good to see you, John. How are you doing?" Dusty crossed the room and gave his friend a warm handshake. His eyes were kind, his expression friendly, easygoing, his smile in full force.

Deb wished he'd look at her like that. Slowly she followed him across the room.

"Saw you two from the window. What happened to Starlight?"

"Stumbled on the way in, think she strained a muscle in that left foreleg. Can I leave her here for a few days?"

"You know you don't have to ask. She's welcome. And who's this pretty miss you've brought? Thought you were bringing the banker."

"Deb, this is John Barrett. John, Deb Harrington *is* the cold, cruel, Scrooge of a hard-hearted banker. D stands for Deb."

"How do you do Mr. Barrett? Ignore Dusty, I'm learning to." She stepped forward and offered her hand.

He struggled to his feet and shook hands with her. His grip was surprisingly strong. He looked tired, old and frail, yet Deb could guess what he looked like before his illness. He was as tall as Dusty, with broad shoulders. His leanness was to excess, but once recovered she thought he would put on weight until he looked as fit as his neighbor.

"Sit down, girl. Can I get you something to drink? You look hot."

Deb flushed, and again regretted not being dressed appropriately. But she didn't want to put this man out. He looked as if he should be in bed resting.

"Dusty'll get us something." John sank back down gratefully.

"Be right back."

His look told Deb to watch herself. He was back with a couple of glasses of cold water almost instantly. He handed one to Deb, one to John, then crossed the room and leaned against the wall near the door.

"This is your business we'll be discussing, Mr. Barrett. If you would rather conduct it in private—" Deb began, glancing at Dusty.

"No, no, that's all right. Hell, Dusty knows all about this. He's the one who got you to come out, right?"

"That's right. I just couldn't refuse his charming invitation."

"That's Dusty. He could charm birds from the trees."

Deb resolutely kept her gaze on the older man. She couldn't stand to see Dusty smirk at his friend's praise.

"We have a serious problem, Mr. Barrett. I need to discuss all the options, to see if we can come up with some kind of solution."

Dusty leaned against the wall some distance away. He could hear everything that was said, but didn't want to interrupt. John could handle his own business. And it was interesting to see Ms. Deb Harrington in action. She reminded him a lot of Marjory, except there was a vulnerability about Deb that Marjory had never had. And an innate sexiness that was driving him slowly crazy. Too caught up in her business dreams, she didn't even seem aware of her appeal to men. Focused on their discussion, she leaned closer to John.

Dusty wondered what she'd look like in the throes of passion. Would she focus totally on the moment, or keep something in reserve? He'd like to see her hair spread out on a pillow, run his fingers through it, feel the silky softness, smell her particular fragrance.

Shifting a bit to ease the growing tightness in his jeans, he tried to think of something else. But time and again his gaze was drawn to Deb. She gestured with her hands, small and graceful with short nails. There was color in her cheeks. He smiled at the sight, remembering the color that had flown there after their kiss last night.

Rubbing his hand across his mouth, he almost imagined he tasted her. She'd been so sweet, so hot. So responsive. And so mad when they'd stopped. She didn't like giving that response. He suspected she liked being in control, all the time. Well, things didn't always go that way. Maybe he'd show her what it was like to have someone else in control, if only for a little while.

He smiled again. There was the ride home ahead of them. He might have called someone from the ranch to pick her up if she hadn't come up with her harebrained suggestion of ordering his hands around. She didn't know cowboys if she thought that would work.

Besides, he deserved something for putting up with her. And a ride with her sharing the saddle was just the reward he would give himself.

"I won't take any more of your time," Deb said gently. "If you could get me copies of those estimates, I'll see what I can do."

"I'll get them out in Monday's mail. Thanks for coming out, Ms. Harrington. Hey, Dusty, thanks for bringing the lady."

"Yeah, you two get things settled?" He pushed off from the wall, every nerve at attention as Deb rose and shook hands with his old friend. She turned and started walking toward him.

Desire slammed in hard. He wanted her. She infuriated him. Her values were screwed up as far as he was concerned. He didn't like her job or her attitude half the time. But the other half was fine. And her sexy walk, the sensual sway of hips, the soft mounds pressing against that cotton shirt, the light in her eyes—all added up to a combustible package. One he wanted to unwrap and savor, however temporarily. He wasn't looking for a long-term commitment, just a night or two in bed together. Like maybe tonight?

"Take it easy, John. I'll call you tomorrow to see how things are going."

"Thanks, Dusty. Do you need a ride home? Lester's around somewhere, he can take you."

"Nah, Deb and I will ride Diego."

"I would love—"

Dusty took her arm and smiled over at John. "See you later." His voice drowned out her protest.

As he pulled her through the front door, she slapped his hand, to no avail. His grip never slackened.

"Dusty, I could get a ride home."

"I'm giving you a ride home." His stride lengthened until she almost ran to keep up. "When I take a girl out, I bring her home."

"Oh, for heaven's sake. This is not some date. Let me get a ride with Lester."

"So?"

"So if I get a ride back with Lester, maybe I can ask him to drop me off in town after I pick up my things."

"What are you talking about?"

"If I get a ride into town, I can get a bus or something back to Denver. Then I don't have to inconvenience any of your employees or stay the entire weekend," she said brightly. Swallowing hard, she smiled up at him, hoping he didn't see how her heartbeat raced at his touch, at his proximity. It would be much safer to get home and away from this sexy cowboy who had her thinking things she had no business thinking.

Dusty looked at her for a long moment, his gaze drawn to the rapid pulse point at her neck. Slowly he smiled and raised his fingers to trace that pounding spot. "I'll take you back to Denver. It's no inconvenience. Ride back with me."

The soft request made her knees buckle. His eyes gazed into hers, warm and amused. She looked away, at his lips. Oops, that was a mistake. Instantly she remembered their kiss.

As if her thoughts were transmitted directly to his mind, he leaned over and brushed her lips with his. "Don't go home just yet, Deb." Another light touch.

She sighed and stepped closer. Something short-circuited in her brain. When he was this close, when he touched her, when he kissed her, nothing computed. She forgot her goals and plans. She wanted to explore this feeling. To sink herself into the sensations he evoked and see where they would lead.

When his mouth covered hers a third time, Deb opened her lips. His tongue brushed against the soft inside of her lower lip, traced her teeth, then slipped in deeper as he gathered her against him. While sweeping the roof of her mouth with his tongue, his arms went around her. Hers encircled his neck and she pressed herself against the long hard length of the man.

It was glorious. Feelings and sensations clashed, built. Desire swept through her, compelling and demanding. She had never felt so attuned to another person. Her body wanted more, her skin craved his touch, her breasts yearned for attention and, deep in her core, something softened, heated, bloomed. Restless, she moved against him, reveling in the groan he responded with.

Heady with feminine power, she knocked off his hat and ran her fingers through his thick hair. Her kisses returned his. She imitated his tongue's tutelage, traced his lips and swept inside. Boldly she met his tongue and began a dance that shook her. Thrust and parry, advance, retreat, swirl and dip. She was shivering with need, burning up with heat. Feeling light-headed, she knew only his mouth anchored her to earth.

When he pulled back, she murmured, "No, no." She wasn't ready to stop. She drew his head back to her aching mouth. She'd never felt so free. She wanted this man like she had never wanted anything before.

Shocked at the thought, she pulled back. Dusty was breathing hard. She was breathing hard. They stood in the open doorway of John Barrett's huge barn for all the world to see.

Aghast, she stepped back, would have stumbled had his hands not been reluctant to let her go.

"I can't believe that," she whispered, appalled at her own behavior. God, she had been plastered to the man. Almost crawling inside him.

"It was pretty earth-shattering," he said, stooping to pick up both hats. He slapped his against his thigh and settled it on his head. Holding out hers, he looked at her, and smiled.

It was the smile that did her in. She took another step back until she felt the doorjamb behind her. A good solid wooden structure that would give her the support she needed, lest she fall on her face.

Gingerly she reached out for the hat, her eyes never leaving his.

"I didn't think you liked me," she said, imitating him by slapping the hat against her thigh, then placing it firmly on her head.

"Honey, what does that have to do with sex?"

She blinked, a sinking feeling growing. He only wanted sex? "Actually, this was a bad idea. I'm here on business—"

Dusty growled as he took a step forward and wrapped his hands around her neck. Using his thumbs beneath her jaw, he tilted her face up to his. "If I hear you say the word 'business' again this weekend, I'm going to get damn mad."

She swallowed, licked her lips. "And what happens if you get damn mad?"

"That depends, which would be worse, no more kisses, or more?"

She couldn't answer. He wasn't hurting her, but she felt every inch of his hands. She liked them on her. Reaching up, she clasped his wrists with her fingers, feeling the rapid rate of his pulse. "You were affected by those kisses as much as I was," she said in wonder. "Your heart is racing."

"Honey, a dead man's heart would pound if you kissed him."

She wrinkled her nose. "Why would I kiss a dead man?"

"Hell if I know, not when you could be kissing me." His kiss was not gentle, but hard and demanding. He pressed her against the wooden frame, one leg pushing between hers. Ducking his head beneath the brim of her hat, he deepened the kiss. Deb could do nothing but hold on as wave after wave of pleasure built.

Abruptly he pulled away, took her by the arm and turned her into the barn.

"Riders coming," he said, glancing over his shoulder as he walked toward Diego.

Deb stumbled, then by sheer determination, strengthened her legs. Thank goodness his hearing was attuned. She would have died of embarrassment if they'd been caught by John Barrett's men.

Dusty tightened the cinch of his horse, checked Starlight one more time, then led Diego from the barn.

Two men rode into the yard. Dusty introduced Deb to Lester and Jack, then swung up onto his horse. He explained why they'd find Starlight in the barn, then smiled.

"Lester, give the lady a hand up, would you? We're riding double back."

"Sure thing, Dusty." The man came up to Deb.

"No, I think—" The last word ended in a scream as Lester picked her up and handed her to Dusty.

"I'm not some doll to be tossed around at your whim," she fumed as Dusty's hard hands gripped her waist.

"Fling your leg over Diego's neck, and don't kick him."

She complied, and sank into the saddle seat, pressed between the horn and the hard male body behind her.

Touching the brim of his hat, Dusty bade the two cowhands goodbye and urged Diego to move out.

Deb tried to hold herself erect, away from the tantalizing chest behind her. Away from the heat that enveloped her even with the inches between them.

"You make me so furious, I could spit," she said. Sitting so far forward in the saddle spread her legs wide. She was conscious of a dampness caused by her reaction to Dusty's kisses. Embarrassed, she wished she'd insisted on a truck. Or she should have just stayed with John Barrett.

"Relax," he said, encircling her waist and pulling her back against him. His arm felt like a hot band of steel. His chest like a wall of molten stone. When his breath brushed across her neck and cheek, she could scarcely breathe.

"I don't think this is such a good idea," she said, fighting every urge in her.

"Why's that?"

"Well, for starters, there is an attraction between us."

"You could say that." He chuckled softly.

"But it can't go anywhere."

"Where do you want it to go?"

"Nowhere. That's just it. I don't live out here, you don't live in Denver. And anyway, we're too different. All you want is sex, and I don't sleep around."

"I'm glad to hear it."

"You are?" She was confused. She thought he wanted to sleep with her.

"Sure, what man wants a woman who shares her charms with everyone?"

"I don't know. But it's not me. I don't ever sleep around. And I don't plan to start now."

He was silent as the horse plodded along. The breeze was light, blowing from the west, drifting with the fragrance of pine and drying grass. The sun had passed its zenith, though there were hours of daylight left. It was warm in the sun, hot where their bodies touched.

"What do you mean?" he said as last, a glimmer of an idea so farfetched he knew he was wrong.

"About what?" She had fallen into the rhythm of the horse, been mesmerized by the beauty of the mountains around them. She loved her home state, and wished now that she ventured outside of Denver a bit more often. This was worth the trip.

"About not ever sleeping around."

"That's pretty clear, I think."

"I think it sounds like never," he said.

She took a deep breath. "That's right."

Feeling his start of surprise, she kept her head straight. She had no reason to be embarrassed. She would feel worse if she slept with every man who ever asked her out. Not that there had been that many—she always made it clear she was focused on her career.

"Well, hell!" he said softly.

The silence stretched as Diego picked his way home. Soon they passed through the fence that separated the two properties.

Deb's thought spun. If she'd known telling a man she was a virgin was such a turnoff, she'd have tried it on the ride in yesterday. She shouldn't have told him. It was not any business of his. Business. Should she mention the word? What would Dusty do if she did? She liked a challenge and he'd thrown one at her when he told her to refrain from saying the B-word again. Careful consideration was needed. Should she deliberately flaunt her fearlessness, or her daring? Or was she really angling for one more kiss before she left?

Once back in Denver, she'd see what she could do for John Barrett, and that would be the end of the matter. There was no other reason for Dusty to seek her out. Maybe if he lived closer...but a four-hour round trip was too much to expect from a casual friend.

Casual? Not with the shimmering awareness that pulsed between them. His arms cloaked her and she felt every muscle move as he rode and guided the horse. The arm across her stomach was a delightful weight that kept her in a constant state of desire. The muscles against her back moved as he reined the horse in, as he leaned over to unlatch and relatch the gate. His breath fanned her cheek, sending tendrils of excitement bubbling through her veins. She was semiaroused just riding the horse while being held as close to Dusty as a lover.

She caught her breath.

"You okay?"

"Yes. How much farther?" Could he feel her heart rate increase? Did he picture them as lovers, tangled in sheets, tangled in each other? She rubbed her palms against her thighs, curling her fingers into a fist to keep from reaching out to touch him.

"Not long. The ride this morning was to show you John's place. The distance between us isn't that far in a straight line."

She arched her back to get a bit of space between them. It rocked her hips further into the saddle, against his rock-hard masculinity.

She flushed and squirmed away.

"Sit still, Deb," Dusty said easily, though there was nothing easy about riding with the woman. He'd been a fool to think of this as a reward. It was hell on earth. The kisses they'd shared had held a lot of promise. But her announcement about her virginity had killed any idea he had of a quick roll in the hay this weekend to get her out of his system. If she'd gone this far in life without a man, she certainly wasn't going to change her style for a cowboy she didn't even like.

He settled her close, ignoring the fact she had to know of his desire. So what? That wouldn't come as a surprise; he'd told her he wanted her. But he also knew when to cut his losses. He'd take her home, thank her for what help she could give to John, and say goodbye.

He kicked Diego to speed up the pace.

"What are you doing? Are we going to gallop?" she asked, clutching his arm.

"Just getting you back a bit faster. I'll take you to Denver tonight. You'll be there before dark, if Diego can get us home quickly."

"Oh." Good. That was what she wanted, right? To go home? To reach her empty, lonely condo tonight. That would give her all day tomorrow to... To what? Go shopping for the few Christmas presents she normally gave. Maybe get a small tree? Read a book? Maybe do laundry? She could treat herself to a show. The important thing was that she would be home. And she would have said goodbye to Dusty Wilson. Once and for all.

Somehow the very thought depressed her.

"If it's truly inconvenient, I could stay," she said unexpectedly.

"It won't be any more inconvenient tonight than tomorrow."

"Fine, then." She sought to memorize every remaining minute. The feel of his thighs against the backs of hers tantalized her beyond bearing. But she would remember. His killer smile drove her to distraction—she would never forget that! Nor the way his kisses had made her feel. Nor the feel of his hands on her. She wished she'd had time for more, but she'd treasure what she'd had. It had been so much more than she ever dreamed of two days ago.

Two days. She didn't think people could pack so much into such a short period of time. Nor feel the ache afterward. How long would she wish for a glimpse of this cowboy? Would she start looking at men on the street, hoping she'd run into him again someday? Or would she quickly forget? He didn't fit with her plan, so move on.

She thought it might be hard to move on.

Even before they rode into the ranch yard, they could smell the smoke and the tantalizing scent of barbecue sauce. Dusty reined Diego to a halt near the corral and studied the small group of people around a huge barbecue pit.

"Ivy!" he roared. She looked up and waved. Dusty maneuvered the horse closer. "What's going on?" Nodding to a couple of the men, he fixed his gaze on Ivy.

"Could ask you the same thing boss. Didn't you leave here this morning with two horses?"

"Starlight's over at John's. She injured a leg. Why the barbecue?"

"Thought we'd have one in honor of our guest. Show her a bit of Western hospitality."

"She lives in Denver, she knows about Western hospitality."

"Not ranch style. Right, hon?" Ivy smiled at Deb, then looked back at Dusty.

"If you hurry, you'll have time to freshen up before the other folks arrive."

"What other folks? Good grief, Ivy, it's almost December. Barbecues are for summer."

"Boss, the weather is almost like summer."

Deb raised her eyebrows. Maybe it was in the fifties, but once the sun set, the temperature would plunge. Not her idea of alfresco weather.

"The hell it is," Dusty said.

"I invited a few neighbors. Thought Deb might want to meet them. They will be funding the payments for John, after all."

"You should have checked with me first. Deb's going back to Denver tonight."

"She can't, everyone is expecting to meet her," Ivy protested.

"Ivy's right," Deb said, delighted with the chance to stay. "She's gone to a lot of trouble. I can stay until tomorrow. And if I get to meet the people who are coming up with the money to pay off the loan, I can add that to my report."

"Hell," Dusty said softly. He turned the horse and headed for the barn. Stopping near the door, he lifted Deb over the saddle horn and let her slide to the ground. Gathering the reins, he glared down at her. The horse shifted impatiently, picking up clues from the rider.

"Might have known you'd find a way to turn what should be a simple party into a business meeting. One day you'll push too far and the backlash won't be pretty."

"Why cowboy, is that a threat?" She placed her hands on her hips and stared up at him with a sassy look. Although her heart was pounding, Deb wondered if she could carry off the bluff. If he moved to dismount, she'd take off like a scared jack rabbit. But with him up on that horse and she on the ground, she felt a modicum of safety. And the impulse to argue wouldn't go away.

Dusty leaned over, his eyes blazing into hers. "Just a promise, sweetcakes. If you're feeling restless, give it a try."

He rode the horse into the barn. For a moment Deb hesitated, then tilting her chin, she followed. No cowboy was going to get the last word with her!

Five

"If you don't like the idea of a barbecue, why not just tell Ivy?" Deb asked, keeping a safe distance.

Dusty dismounted, his eyes narrowing. "I don't mind. Gives me a chance to visit with friends."

"You didn't seem pleased with Ivy."

"Thought you were in a hurry to get back," he said.

He didn't want her staying. He was angry that his plans to get rid of her had been upset by Ivy's impromptu party. She should have guessed.

"Maybe I can catch a ride into town and get a bus back, or something."

"I don't think so. I brought you, I'll take you home."

"Just like with the horse," she said.

"Exactly." He slung the heavy saddle over his shoulder as if it weighed nothing, led the horse into the corral, then headed for the tack room.

Deb followed.

He paused in the opening. "Hadn't you better go do something about getting ready?"

"Are you sure?"

"Hell, I'm not sure about anything right now." He dumped the saddle on a rack, and lifted his hat to run his fingers through his hair. Slanting her a look, he shrugged. "Just try to remember you're not at your fancy bank here, Deb. These are good people, but not ones to put on airs to. Wear your hair down and enjoy yourself."

"Fine." She spun around and headed for the house, her cheeks burning. She did not put on airs! If he thought that, he didn't know her at all. And why should she care? She would be gone tomorrow. Never see the man again. And good riddance!

Standing in front of her mirror half an hour later, Deb tried to see what Dusty saw when he looked at her. She'd brushed her hair out until it shone. Bringing the sides and top up in a high ponytail, she'd left the back to hang down below her shoulders. A light touch of makeup and she was set. She'd gotten off the worst of the dust from her jeans and shoes and changed into a pink turtleneck. If it didn't get too cold, she'd be fine with just her jacket. And if the night grew cold, Deb thought they'd move into the bunkhouse or barn to stay warm.

Quelling the butterflies in her stomach, she raised her chin and headed outside. Eight years of business hadn't cured her of the nerves that hit anytime she faced crowds. She was shy, and worked hard to overcome her feelings of inadequacy when in a large group. This proved to be much more of an ordeal for her than Dusty could imagine. She wished she had gone home after all.

Walking to the flat area beyond the bunkhouse, she counted the number of people gathered. It looked like a huge crowd, but calmly she focused on the different faces. There were only thirty, not hundreds. Still, a large group when she knew no one. And more coming. A truck pulled in and a couple quickly slammed the doors and hastened to the mingling crowd, smiles broad.

Old friends, she mused, her pace slowing even more. Everyone seemed to know everyone else. As each truck pulled into the yard, its passengers were quickly welcomed. Hugs ex-

changed, kisses shared, smiles of delight and laughing greet-
ings seemed the norm. Taking a deep breath, Deb continued
walking.

"Hey, Deb, over here," Ivy called. Deb's smile felt pasted
on, but she obediently changed direction, glad for one familiar,
friendly face.

In moments she had met a dozen people, men and women.
She'd been handed a beer from one friendly cowboy, who then
proceeded to invite her to a barn dance the next weekend.

"Oh, I don't think barn dances are Deb's thing," Dusty
said, coming up behind her and putting an arm around her
shoulders.

Too startled to protest, Deb looked at him in surprise.

"Right, sweetcakes?" he asked, grinning that lopsided
smile that had her knees buckling and her heart tripping up in
her throat.

"So, you and Deb are an item," the cowboy said, shaking
his head sadly. "I'm always too late."

"We're not an item," she said quickly. Is that what everyone thought?

"She's just visiting for the weekend," Dusty clarified, his
fingers rubbing gently against the soft skin of her neck beneath
her fall of hair. It felt like velvet, as soft as a horse's nose.
He liked the silky feel of her hair against the back of his hand.
And she fit right beneath his arm, as if she'd been made for
him.

Right—maybe if he wore a three-piece suit every day and
could total numbers in his head.

"Dusty, hi, we just got here." A bright, sassy-looking red-
head hurried over and reached up to kiss him on the cheek.

"Hi, Joan. Good to see you. Where's Tim?"

Grinning up at him, she shrugged. "Probably by the beer.
Thanks for asking us. I was getting crazy, we haven't been
anywhere in weeks. And if the weather changes and snow
starts to come, we could be stuck at home for months!"

"I'll have to speak to Tim for you."

"Don't you dare. He does his best to keep me happy."

"From the radiant look you always have, he succeeds," Dusty teased.

She nodded with a big grin, her eyes shifting to Deb.

"Hello." Offering her hand, she smiled warmly. "Didn't mean to interrupt anything, but I haven't seen this fellow in ages. I'm Joan Silver. We live on a ranch the other side of town."

"Hello." Deb shook her hand. "I'm Deb Harrington, from Denver."

"From the big bad bank in Denver that's trying to take John's ranch," Dusty said, only half teasing. He was still riled she hadn't made a decision.

"How's John doing?"

"Pretty good. We were over there earlier."

"And I told you no decision's been made, so don't go blaming me again," Deb added.

Dusty moved his fingers again, beneath that glorious blond hair. He'd seen the single men eyeing her, even a couple of the married ones. Mad as he was about the situation with John, he planned to stake some sort of claim on her in front of his neighbors. She was his guest for the weekend, and he wanted to make sure everyone knew it. Including Deb Harrington.

"John just had a run of bad luck. He'll come around," Joan said. "Oh, I better go say hi to Ivy or I'll be last to eat." She smiled and hurried across to where Ivy put plates and utensils on the makeshift serving table.

"I thought you wanted me to forget about the bank for a while," Deb said, pulling away from Dusty. "Yet you keep bringing it up."

"I can't seem to help myself," he said. "It's the reason you're here. Otherwise why would I have insisted you come meet John?"

"I came because you made threats. Just to be bossy and throw your weight around."

"Ah, sweetcakes, if I hadn't, you wouldn't have come."

"My coming still might not change anything."

"If you decide to proceed with the foreclosure, I'll still speak to your boss," he warned.

Deb looked as if he'd slapped her. For a moment Dusty wavered, then firmed his resolve. John was an old and long-time friend. Dusty would do all he could to make sure the man didn't lose his place. He'd only just met Deb. Granted he was attracted to her, but that was purely physical. He refused to throw away a friendship for a toss in the hay.

"You must do what you think is best, but if we do proceed, it will be because it is in the best interest of the bank, and I think my boss will back me up on it."

Touching the tip of her nose lightly, he grinned down at her. "But you're not sure, are you, sweetcakes?"

"Stop calling me that."

Smiling, he took her arm. "Let's mingle a bit, have you meet some more of my neighbors. Enjoy what you can of the weekend. You'll be back in Denver tomorrow."

He wasn't sure, but every indication showed him she wasn't confident of her boss's backing. He knew he'd back his employees to the limit, and every one of them knew it, as well. Made him glad he wasn't in the cutthroat corporate world. How did Deb stand it?

As Deb licked her fingertips from the last of her barbecued ribs, she wondered when she'd had as much fun. Thinking back, one or two times in college sprang to mind. But since then, nothing. She laughed at the tall tales the cowboys told, listened, fascinated, to the hardships some of the women had endured, intrigued they could make it seem like an adventure. It reminded her of an old-fashioned sitcom, in which everyone liked everyone else, everyone got along, shared good times and bad. This was a close-knit group. Enviously, she studied Dusty and his interaction with his neighbors. He seemed at ease with the women as well as the men. Obviously respected in the area, when asked his opinion, the men listened. The women—married and single—flirted and he gave back as good as he got, but only on a lighthearted, superficial level. Something told Deb he never took much of anything seriously. Just like her father. And, like her father, he could be just as charming to everyone.

Yet Dusty did it in such a manner, no one could accuse him of leading them on. As much as she might wish to level that charge against him, she couldn't. He'd been more than forthright in telling her what he didn't like about her. Then confusing her to bits by kissing her like there was no tomorrow. Was that how he handled everything? With passion and zest? Yes, that and a laid back charm that baffled her. His ranch seemed a mix of ruin and success. While the house appeared shabby, needed repairs and painting, the bunkhouse kitchen sparkled and contained the latest appliances. The barn had a new roof, but the siding gapped and needed painting. Dusty acted as though he didn't care much one way or the other about things. He certainly didn't run a tight ship.

She was out of her element. The sooner she got home, the better.

"Enjoying yourself, hon?" Ivy sat beside her in the seat Dusty had just vacated, a fragrant cup of coffee cradled in her strong hands. Bright lights illuminated the yard. The air felt crisp and cool, but not uncomfortably cold.

"I sure am. Thank you for this, Ivy. I can't remember when I've had such a good time."

Ivy beamed. Looking around the group scattered all over, balancing plates in laps, sipping brew and coffee, laughing, she nodded. "It was a good idea. I'm glad you got to meet some other folks. Help balance that life you live in Denver."

Deb smiled. "I live a fine life in Denver, just what I want."

"So, tell me a bit more. I've never lived in a big city. I like ranch life, and Hank and I chose this way a long time ago."

"I was born and raised in Denver, so it's all I know. I worked hard to get my job, now I work hard to keep it." There wasn't much to tell about her life—at least to interest these ranching folks.

"Want to be head banker one day?" Ivy asked.

"President? Yes, I'd like that. But right now, I'm aiming for a vice presidency."

"Think you'll make it?" Ivy's questions were blunt, but her interest sincere.

"I don't know," Deb confessed, looking away. "It's really

a man-oriented industry, even though women are making in-roads. My boss is not particularly supportive of women in management. He thinks we should all be tellers."

"Heard of men like that."

"Men like what?" Dusty asked. In his hands were two plates piled high with chocolate cake and vanilla ice cream. He handed one to Deb, rested his foot against the edge of her bench and set to eating.

"Chauvinistic men who think a woman's place is in the home," Ivy drawled as if teasing him.

"Mmm, could be a point in that," he said, his eyes dancing in amusement.

"When have you ever thought so?" she asked.

"I'd say all the time," Deb volunteered, meeting his gaze with a questioning one of her own.

"No, I don't mind women working. Got to do something besides make beds and do dishes—unless they like doing that kind of thing, like you do, Ivy."

"Good recovery, boss. Go on, I'm atwitter to hear what you have to say next."

"You know damn well how I feel about women and work," Dusty said. He looked at Deb. "I don't mind women working. It's when they become obsessed with their job to the detriment of everything else that I object. In fact, I object to that in anyone, man or woman."

Deb dropped her gaze to the slowly softening ice cream. She took a bite and let it melt in her mouth as she contemplated whether or not Dusty would consider her obsessed with her work. To some degree, maybe. But it was because she was so determined to escape her childhood. She wanted to make something of herself. To know she could support herself in the style she liked, and not ever be beholden to some man. Never be forced to live a way she didn't want because of lack of money or security.

"Ring any bells, Deb?" Dusty asked.

She glanced up. "Actually I don't obsess about my job, but I do about chocolate. This cake is delicious." She forked another bite.

"Glad you like it, hon. Well, if Dusty's back to staking his claim, I'll mosey along. I've known all about three's a crowd for a long time."

For a moment it was just the two of them. Deb concentrated on her cake.

"Glad you stayed?" Dusty asked, taking the spot Ivy left.

"Yes. This has been fun."

"What do you do for fun in Denver, Deb?" he asked, setting his plate on the grass beneath the bench and turning a bit. He still wore his hat and tipped it so it sat on the back of his head.

She noticed how he used that hat to reflect his moods. Pushed back like that, he was at his friendliest. Smiling, she took another bite of cake and thought of how to answer him. Whatever she said, it didn't compare to this, and he would know it.

"I like quiet things, like going to the movies. I have dinner with friends. In the winter I sometimes go skiing."

"Involved with any man?"

She looked up at him from beneath her lashes. "And if I said I was?" she asked.

He leaned over until his nose almost touched hers. His blue eyes filled her vision and her breath caught in her throat. The hustle and activity around them faded as she only saw Dusty.

"I'd say you're playing with fire kissing me if someone's waiting for you. I also think there's not. You have a bit more integrity than to cheat."

She warmed at his words. At least he thought enough of her to say that.

"No, there's no man." Of course he knew that from their conversation that afternoon. There had never been a man—not in the way Dusty meant.

"Why not?" He leaned back.

Grateful for the breathing space, she finished the last of the cake.

"I'm busy at work. Then tired in the evenings."

"Come on, Deb, you're too young to be that tired. Even if you were, you have the weekends."

She shrugged, leaned over and placed her empty plate beneath the bench as Dusty had done.

"Tell me about your folks," he said.

"They're dead," she said flatly. The last thing she wanted to do was talk about her parents. Desperately she looked around. She could join that group near the corral, they were having a good time, laughing and talking—not interrogating each other.

"Recently?" he asked, pushing even though he recognized her slammed door.

"Not recently enough, okay?" She rose and headed for the corral. She wanted laughter and fun, not a trip down memory lane.

Dusty watched her march off. So, Miss Businesswoman Personified had an off limits on her parents. Why? he wondered. She couldn't miss them so much she couldn't talk about them, not with that last remark. His gut tightened. Had they abused her as a child? He couldn't imagine anything worse. And especially not to a pretty feminine woman like Deb. Or was it just some family feud that lingered?

He rose, determined to find out more. But not tonight. Tonight he wanted her to enjoy herself. He suspected she didn't do it enough.

It was late by the time the last neighbor tooted his horn and drove off. Time had flown by. After dinner, the women had helped Ivy with the dishes. Deb had enjoyed the camaraderie in the kitchen. Not once had they made her feel like an outsider, including her in their banter and jokes. The chore had been finished in record time, Deb thought. Especially with so many different women invading Ivy's domain.

When the talk had turned to Christmas, of what they were serving for dinner or what presents they still had to get, Deb had grown quiet. She enjoyed listening to stories about other families, and wistfully wondered if she'd ever have one of her own. For the most part, Christmas was a lonely day for her.

Once darkness fell, everyone had drawn closer to the barbecue pit for the warmth. Conversations ranged from ranching business, to vacation spots and the barn dance scheduled to take place next weekend. Dusty had found her and sat beside her, but refrained from casual touches, careful to keep several inches between them. She'd almost regretted walking away from him earlier, but she would not stand to be questioned about her past.

And it didn't matter. After tomorrow, she'd be gone.

"Enjoy yourself?" Dusty asked as the last car disappeared down the driveway. The cowboys headed for the bunkhouse, Ivy and Hank wandered toward their cottage.

"I had a nice time," Deb said primly. She wanted to say more, but refused to do anything that would open the conversation again.

"Come on, I'll get the lights." He took her arm, sliding his hand down to grasp her hand. Lacing his fingers through hers, he headed for the dark house.

She walked quickly, keeping pace with him. Her emotions began to spin again. Just from holding his hand! Tightening her fingers, she tried to imprint the feel of his rough and callused palm against hers, the strength of his hand that held hers so gently. She remembered wondering about how it would feel when she met him. His rough calluses evoked a flurry of sensations that were difficult to define. He was a strong, hard man—one a woman could depend on. He proved such a contradiction. She wondered if she would ever understand him.

Dusty let go when he opened the front door. When he flicked on the light, he motioned her to enter the house. "Sleep in as late as you like tomorrow. When you've finished breakfast, I'll take you back to Denver."

"Thank you. And thanks again for all—"

"Don't thank me, Deb. I want you to stop the foreclosure on John's house. Nothing more."

"I can't guarantee that."

"I know. Good night." He strode past her, down the hall to the office.

Deb watched him, hurt that he'd brushed aside her thanks. She'd had a fun evening, one of the best she could remember, but he didn't want to hear it. And he made it clear that everything had been done solely with the thought of getting John off the hook. Nothing was personal. Not even his kisses?

She shook her head, tilted up her chin and climbed the stairs. For all she knew, that could be part of his campaign. Have her fall for him so she wouldn't foreclose.

No, she wasn't falling for him, for heaven's sake, so that didn't even come into play. She'd visited, she'd return home and evaluate everything she'd seen. Then make her decision.

The ride into Denver seemed to fly by. Dusty played his country music, Deb watched as the distant silhouette of the tall buildings of downtown drew closer and closer. She wanted to say something, but didn't know what. She could make him much more approachable if she'd just tell him she'd hold off on John's foreclosure, but she wasn't sure she could. There was her responsibility to the bank to consider. For the first time since she started work, her job presented a personal dilemma.

It seemed like no time before Dusty pulled up in front of her condo complex. Deb was not ready to face her empty home.

"I could fix you some lunch," she said.

"No, thanks. I've got to get back." He opened the door, took her small case from the truck bed and headed for her front door.

She grabbed her briefcase, the one she'd never opened the entire time she was at the ranch and followed. He set her case on the stoop.

"Thanks for the weekend, Dusty. Now I've been on a ranch, learned to ride a horse, and met cowboys." She smiled, desperately hoping the loneliness she feared didn't show in her expression. She hadn't even been gone forty-eight hours. She'd had a nice visit, met some new people, had some new experiences. Nothing major had changed.

"Goodbye, Deb." He leaned over and brushed his lips against hers, then turned and headed toward his truck.

He was gone inside ten seconds.

"And he never looked back," she said slowly. When the truck turned the corner, Deb turned to unlock her door.

During the next few days Deb had trouble concentrating. She'd be in the middle of a financial analysis and remember Ivy's insisting Dusty clear his own plate. Or she'd remember the feelings that coursed through her when they'd rode double on Dusty's big gelding. Sometimes she'd smile at the jokes that had flown fast and furious at the barbecue. Mostly, however, she relived Dusty's kisses.

During the nights, dreams danced through her head, of Dusty coming to take her to his room, of wild nights in tangled sheets. She'd awaken each morning chagrined at having another dream that had her longing for things that would never be. Longing for the attention of a laid-back, charm-your-socks-off cowboy, who thought businesswomen were only slightly higher than locoweed in the scale of things.

Friday afternoon, Annalise sauntered into Deb's office, carrying a stack of letters.

"This is the last of the dictation for the week. Did you decide to clear out your In box for a reason?" She placed the stack of pristine letters in the center of the desk and sank into the visitor's chair.

"Was it more than normal?" Deb asked absently. She pushed aside the annual report she'd been skimming and took up her pen. Signing her name on each letter, she didn't bother reading them. Annalise was a perfectionist.

"Hot date tonight?" Annalise asked.

"No." No date, hot or otherwise. But what else was new? "You?"

"Yep, this guy's a real babe. He works across town in the D.A.'s office."

"How did you meet him?" Deb listened with only half an ear as she signed the correspondence. This was the last of the things on her desk. For once she was totally caught up. Something even Phil Moore had noticed when he'd stopped by to chat one day. Working late each night had accomplished it. And that had beat going home to an empty condo. Somehow after the excitement of last weekend, her place had seemed too quiet, too lonely.

"He knows Derek. You know, the cop I date sometimes."

"How do you keep them all straight?" Deb asked as she signed the last letter. The normal sense of accomplishment was missing. How odd. She'd done tons more work this week than recently, both Phil and Mr. Montgomery knew it, and it all left her feeling vaguely dissatisfied.

And she still hadn't made a decision on John Barrett's loan.

Annalise giggled. "You're funny, Deb. Every man out there is totally different. I don't have any trouble."

"And none of them mind that you're playing the field?"

"I'm not ready to get serious. I want to be like you and get somewhere before tying myself down to some man. I figure when you get the V.P. slot, they'll have to hire someone to fill your place, and maybe that will leave an opening somewhere I can slide into. One day, I want the job you have now, maybe even become a vice president. By then you'll be president and a lot more encouraging to women than old Montgomery is."

"Hush, Mr. Montgomery is the president now and deserves our loyalty if not our liking."

"Come on, Deb, it's just you and me. Give the corporate line to those who might believe it, but don't buy into it yourself. This is just a job. And he's one chauvinistic jerk who likes to throw his weight around."

"I'll keep that in mind," Deb said dryly.

Annalise grinned. "I bet. See you on Monday. Don't do anything I wouldn't do."

"Well, that leaves the field wide open," Deb murmured when Annalise closed the door behind her.

Actually, she would probably do everything Annalise wouldn't do—like vacuum her place, do laundry, maybe bake some Christmas cookies. She bet Annalise had never spent a weekend alone in her life!

Sighing, Deb rose. It was Friday, time she should be looking forward to. Instead she delayed her departure as long as she could. There was nothing to hurry home for.

* * *

Dusty drummed his fingers against the steering wheel and looked at his watch again. Damn, where was she? His watch showed almost five-thirty. How late did she work on a Friday?

Of course she could have made plans, gone somewhere straight from work. He hoped she hadn't. Maybe he should have called. But he hadn't made up his mind to come until just a few hours ago. Or was he fooling himself?

He'd thought about Deb all week. Sometimes the memories made him mad, but more and more he remembered the feel of her in his arms on Diego's back. The taste of her when he kissed her. The movement of her body against his as she kissed him back. Hell, just as every other time, thinking about her made him want her.

Where was she?

He spotted her old car long before she saw him. Of course he had been on the lookout for her, while she wouldn't suspect he'd show up again on Friday night. He glanced at his watch. It was after five-thirty. Not so late, unless someone had arrived before five.

He climbed out of the truck and headed for her front door as she turned into the short driveway beside her condo. He saw the surprise on her face. Were any of the expressions chasing around ones of gladness to see him?

Deb caught her breath when she saw the old truck. There were dozens—hundreds—of old trucks on the roads. When Dusty climbed out, her heart soared. For some reason, Dusty Wilson was on her doorstep again. Slowly she smiled.

"Hey, sweetcakes, how are you?" he called as she stepped out of the car.

She left her briefcase, grabbed her purse and slammed the door. Stomping around the car and heading for her front door, she tried to be annoyed by the casual endearment. But her heart pumped away, and the happiness that settled over her was almost scary.

"My name's Deb," she said, climbing the two steps until she stood close enough to feel his body heat, to smell the fragrance of horse, leather and Dusty himself. She looked up; even wearing high heels, he towered over her.

"Yeah, sweetcakes, I know." Without thought, he lowered his face. His mouth captured hers in a kiss that was both impatient and thorough.

Scarcely breathing, she leaned into him. It had been so long. And she had thought it might be forever. Feeling giddy as a schoolgirl, she opened her mouth and gave herself up to pure pleasure.

Several long minutes later she realized they were standing on her front porch, in plain sight of all her neighbors. Fortunately it was almost dark and she had not left her porch light on. Pushing against his shoulder, she broke contact.

"What are you doing here?" she asked breathlessly. Fumbling for her keys, she was both relieved and annoyed when Dusty took them and effortlessly opened her door. He ushered her inside, and closed it behind him. Tossing his hat onto a nearby table, he reached for her again.

"Wait, Dusty—"

But he'd waited a week, and that was all he was willing to wait. His left hand pressed her against him while his right released her hair from the tight French braid she insisted on wearing. When it came loose, he threaded his fingers through the softness and held her head for his kisses.

She looked so prim in her business suit, and felt as hot as fire in his arms. Her hands moved across his shoulders, down his biceps, as if learning every inch of him. He liked it, wanted more. He wanted to feel her skin against his, have those fingers tease and provoke every inch of him.

And he wanted to do the same thing to her. He wanted to taste her, kiss her, touch every single inch.

Shaken at the strength of his feelings, he pushed back, gulping in air. She would make a man forget his name.

Slowly, Deb lifted her eyelids, gazed at him. Blood pounded through her, every cell clamored for more. His kisses could turn her to mush. What would making love be like?

"What are you doing here?" she repeated.

"I had some unfinished business to attend to," he said. He

hoped she wouldn't ask what. He didn't want to tell her she was his unfinished business. All week long he'd thought about her. Maybe this weekend he'd get enough of her to cool down.

"I see." She smoothed her jacket, tried to get her galloping senses under some control. Wetting her lips, she tasted him, and her heart thumped. She wanted to be cool, collected, though it was damn hard after his greeting. Acting like a crazy schoolgirl with a major crush would never do.

He looked down at her. "Didn't bring any work home, I see."

She shook her head, ignoring the briefcase in the car with the case folders she had planned to review.

"What did you decide about John?"

There it was—his unfinished business. She had wondered how long it would take him to bring that up. It was the only thing between them, after all. Except for some very potent kisses.

"It looks as if I can extend the loan for a while. And if your friends are sincere in making a partial payment on the amount in arrears, we can settle everything in another week or so."

He nodded and looked around.

For a moment Deb followed his gaze, wondering what he thought as he checked out her place. She had taken time to buy the best she could afford. Each piece had been lovingly chosen for her house. The Queen Anne furniture was dainty and esthetically pleasing. The brocades rich and formal. Nothing reminded her of the apartment on Pearl Street. Nothing reminded her of her barren childhood.

"Is that why you stopped by, to ask about Mr. Barrett?" she asked as Dusty wandered around the living room, touching a figurine, studying the paintings she'd acquired.

"Nope, I came to see if you'd like to go back to the ranch with me for the weekend."

Six

"**I** can't go to the ranch with you," Deb said.

"Why not? Big plans this weekend?"

She opened her mouth to say yes, then promptly closed it. She didn't have *any* plans for the weekend, unless she went Christmas shopping. Not that she had to let him know that. Though Dusty seemed smart enough to guess. Slowly she shook her head.

"Great, change into your jeans and let's go."

"I can't," she repeated.

"Why not?"

"Why are you asking me?" she asked suspiciously. "It seemed to me last weekend you couldn't wait to get rid of me. You weren't too happy about that impromptu barbecue because you were stuck with my company for that much longer."

Slowly he smiled, and her heart skidded. "Last weekend was business. You've decided to delay the foreclosure until we can get the money together, so this weekend will be purely pleasure."

She shivered as his words evoked visions of the kind of pleasure she'd like to receive from Dusty over the weekend.

"Nothing's firm yet with John Barrett," she said, torn. She wanted to go. She didn't want to go. She was afraid of where her feelings were leading her. And that could be a danger she dare not risk. She would not allow herself to fall for some charming cowboy with a devastating smile.

He shrugged. "Get changed."

She hesitated for only a second. She really did want to go. "Okay. Wait here."

He looked around the living room. "I'll check out your place. Hurry up."

"I'm hungry. Can we get something to eat before leaving?" She had skipped lunch again, and couldn't last until they reached the ranch.

"We'll go for pizza."

Deb nodded and hurried down the hall to her room. Closing the door behind her, she was extremely conscious of Dusty in her home. Seeing him had come as a shock, she had heard nothing from him in the week since she'd last seen him, had not expected to see him again. Unless something went wrong with the way she handled John Barrett's situation, of course. Then she could expect him to ride in with guns blazing.

Quickly taking off her suit and blouse, she began to change.

Dusty watched Deb hurry down the hall, wishing for a moment he'd offered to help her change. Smiling at the picture of outrage that popped into his mind, he walked into her living room and stared around him. She had some beautiful pieces of furniture, every single one brand new. The few knickknacks on her tables were delicate crystal or fine china. The paintings on the walls were original oils. He studied the outdoor scenes—English gardens for the most part. Feminine, delicate, romantic—all reflecting Deb's taste. No wonder she found the ranch so different.

Nothing he owned compared with what she had. The old sofa in his living room had been used when his uncle bought it twenty years ago. The chairs were scuffed and scarred, though too comfortable to toss. And every window in the house could use new curtains.

He felt uncomfortable in the decidedly feminine room. It wasn't the furnishings, but the knowledge that she was so like his ex-wife. Material things were obviously important to Deb. She worked long and hard for the success that could guarantee this kind of lifestyle. He didn't want any part of it. He liked working with the land, pitting himself against nature and sometimes coming up a winner. The men he worked with were friends as well as employees. Fellow ranchers shared his interests and triumphs as well as defeats. There wasn't anything he'd change, not for Marjory, and certainly not for Deb Harrington.

But that didn't ease the sweep of desire he experienced every time he saw her.

When he heard her in the hall, he turned, prepared this time for the reaction of his body when she came into view. Steeling himself to give nothing away, he stepped forward, running his gaze from her throat over her softly rounded breasts to her narrow waist. Her curvy hips were outlined by those damn tight jeans again. He swallowed and met the uncertainty in her eyes.

"I don't know about this, Dusty," she said. "No pressure about John Barrett?"

"Now why would I put any pressure on you, sweetcakes? You said you'd practically decided to delay any action until we had a chance to get all the money together."

"I know I said that. The question is, can I trust you?"

He smiled and nodded, grabbing her around the waist and hauling her to him. She tilted her head back, exposing her throat, but held her ground. With a groan, Dusty lowered his mouth to that silky skin and kissed her, licked her, opened his lips and tasted her. Moving to the pulse point that throbbed in her neck, he rested his lips on it, counting the cadence until it raced. Moving to her jaw, he nipped her, then moved to find her waiting lips.

Deb thought she'd died and gone to heaven. Dusty's mouth was hot, as were the tingles coursing through her. Unable to keep her balance, she reached out to hold on to something solid—Dusty. When his mouth found hers, she sighed, closed her eyes and gave herself up to the delight that swamped her. It felt so good, so right, to be held by a man, to have that man kiss her and touch her like she was precious.

Ever since last Sunday, she'd wanted more kisses. She had tried to deny it to herself, had tried to pretend it didn't matter if he never called, never came to see her again, but she'd been lying. For once she allowed herself to revel in the sensations that shimmered through her. The blood pounding in her veins spread the heat throughout her body. Dusty's tongue found hers, danced, enticed, tantalized. She mimicked him, followed into his mouth, tasting him, learning every millimeter of that cavern. His lips were hard and warm and demanding.

Desperate for breath, Deb pulled back an inch, gasping for air. Her hands held on tightly, her body pressed intimately against his, every inch blazing with awareness and yearnings.

"I think we'll never leave if we don't go soon," she said breathlessly, not relinquishing her hold a mite.

He smiled and drew his fingers through her hair. "Maybe, but there's no rush."

Reluctantly disengaging herself, she stepped back, and looked up at him with wary eyes. Had she misread the situation?

"Just what are you expecting this weekend?" she asked cautiously.

Dusty stared at her for a moment. "What do you think, Deb? I asked you to come to the ranch for some fun, to give you a change from Denver. I didn't say anything about joining me in my bed. Though if you wanted that as part of it, I wouldn't say no."

"Well, that's up front and blunt," she said, trying to ignore the shiver of excitement his words sparked.

"Are we going to play games now? I think we're past that. I want you, there's no big secret about it. And from your responses to our kisses, I don't think you're totally indifferent."

She shook her head. "Not indifferent, but not interested."

PLAY
ROMANCE
ROULETTE

Try your luck at our "Casino" and claim Free Books & a Free Mystery Gift

Turn the page to play Roulette!...

PLAY

ROMANCE ROULETTE

NO COST OR OBLIGATION - EVER!

HOW TO PLAY:

1. Flip your lucky coin in the air and then use it to scratch off the silver panel on the Roulette Wheel opposite. Match the number you reveal against the claim chart beneath to see how many FREE GIFTS you can claim.

2. When you send back this card you will receive specially selected Silhouette® novels from the Desire™ series and a mystery gift. These books and gift are yours to keep absolutely FREE

3. And there's no catch. You're under no obligation to buy anything. We charge you nothing for your first shipment. And you don't have to make a minimum number of purchases - not even one.

4. The fact is that thousands of readers enjoy receiving books by post from the Reader Service. They like the convenience of home delivery and they like getting the best new novels at least a month before they are available in the shops. And of course, postage and packing is COMPLETELY FREE!

5. We hope that after receiving your free books you'll want to remain a subscriber. But the choice is yours - to continue or cancel at any time. So why not take up our invitation with no obligation of any kind - you'll be glad you did!

So go ahead.
Play "Romance Roulette" now and claim everything you're entitled to!

We all love mysteries… so as well as your free books, there may also be an intriguing gift waiting for you! Simply scratch away the silver panel and check the claim chart to see what you can receive.

CLAIM CHART

7 RED — **FOUR FREE BOOKS** & A FREE MYSTERY GIFT

11 BLACK — **FOUR FREE BOOKS**

5 RED — **THREE FREE BOOKS**

21 BLACK — **TWO FREE BOOKS**

Scratch here to reveal where the Roulette Ball landed

D8LI

YES! I have scratched away the silver panel on the Roulette Wheel. Please send me all the FREE gifts for which I qualify. I understand that I am under no obligation to purchase any books as explained on the opposite page and overleaf. I am over 18 years of age.

MRS/MS/MISS/MR _____ INITIALS _____

BLOCK CAPITALS PLEASE

SURNAME _____

ADDRESS _____

_____

POSTCODE _____

▶ DETACH AND POST CARD TODAY. NO STAMP NEEDED ▶

THE READER SERVICE™
FREEPOST SEA3794
CROYDON
Surrey
CR9 3AQ

If offer card is missing, write to: The Reader Service, P.O. Box 236, Croydon, Surrey CR9 3RU.

"Couldn't prove it by those kisses."

"Not interested in a long-term relationship," she clarified.

"How about a short-term fling?"

She was tempted, oh, so tempted. But resolutely, she shook her head. "I have my career to worry about right now. I need to be focused on that."

"Right, I know how much emphasis career women place on their jobs. At least we're square on that. Is that little bag all you're bringing?" The coolness of his tone sharply contrasted with the warmth of his embrace.

"Yes." She should refuse to go. His good mood had shattered with her last comment. Though, knowing Dusty, he would be in high spirits soon. Nothing fazed him—just like her ne'er-do-well father. Live for the moment and hang the future. Enjoy life and don't sweat the small stuff. Like a job, or a home.

"Come on, sweetcakes, let's go get some pizza."

Despite her misgivings, Deb's heart lifted. She was going away for the weekend. For a moment she almost felt like Annalise, a swinging woman of the nineties. She'd have something to talk about on Monday. It wasn't quite the same kind of weekends Annalise experienced, but it was as daring as Deb got. She'd enjoy herself and keep Dusty Wilson at arm's length.

"I know the perfect place," she said, unable to contain the giddy sense of anticipation.

It was noisy, crowded and hot. A counter was all that separated the kitchen from the dining area. Families occupied almost every table, with children ranging from infants in carrier seats to teenagers huddled over the video games. The jukebox blared some fast rock-and-roll number and the counter people called orders out without a mike.

Dusty leaned over to be heard above the din and said, "You've shocked me, sweetcakes. This is nothing like I thought you'd pick. I thought we'd hit some staid quiet Italian place that also serves up pizza."

"I always buy my pizza here," she said primly. Her eyes

swept the room. While she had bought pizza here, she had never stayed to eat it, always taking it home to eat in solitary silence. Often while waiting for her order to be cooked, she'd wistfully watched families sharing, laughing, fussing. One of her secret wishes had been to come here and eat—not alone but with someone.

Dusty looked around and shook his head. "What do you want?"

"Pepperoni, sausage and mushrooms."

"Beer to drink?" he asked.

She nodded, suddenly feeling as tongue-tied as a teenager on her first date. Maybe this hadn't been the place to come. Maybe she should have just ordered something to be delivered to her house. Maybe—

Dusty took her arm and turned her toward the dining room, one hand holding the pitcher of beer. Two mugs hung from his thumb. "Where do you want to sit?"

She looked at the few empty tables. The one in the corner would offer the greatest distance from the laughing teenagers. Maybe they could hear each other better there. She headed for it.

Dusty set the pitcher and glasses down, poured the beer, then moved his chair close to hers and sat down.

She looked at him—he sat close enough that she could feel the radiant heat from his body, could smell his male scent. Wanting to lean closer, Deb resisted, kept her distance. Nervously she reached for the beer, took a sip.

"Come here a lot, do you?" Dusty said, leaning back in his chair, pushing his hat back on his head as he surveyed the room.

"A couple of times a month," Deb said, tracing the condensation on her glass. She wasn't about to tell him she never stayed.

"Got any quarters?"

She blinked. Where had that come from? "I guess."

"Check it out. The jukebox is finished and we can choose our own songs."

Deb fished out three quarters and handed them to Dusty.

His hand closed over hers and he hauled her after him as he crossed the crowded pizza parlor. Skimming the list of songs, Deb realized she didn't know half of them.

"What do you want to hear?"

"You decide," she said, studying the blend of selections from country to rock to gospel.

She watched as he punched in the letters and numbers for a wide assortment of country music. In seconds the voice she'd heard in the truck last week blared across the speakers. Again she listened to the list the woman had of what a man of hers would have to do. Again she wished she had a man that considered he belonged to her.

"No suits," Dusty said as they dodged kids and pizza-laden parents on their way back to their table.

"What?"

"Not a single person in here is wearing a suit. Does that make you feel odd?" he asked, holding her chair out for her, then sitting much too close.

"Should it?"

"Doesn't fit my image of you."

"Maybe your image is warped by your ex-wife," she snapped, suddenly aware that this was not the kind of place she ever ate in. It suited her for take-out, but she would feel odd wearing her business suit among the casual families.

Dusty leaned his arm against the back of her chair, hot and hard as it pressed against the back of her shoulders. Deb debated sitting forward, but she liked the feeling. She remained where she was, trying to separate the tingling sensations from the mundane conversation. It was like trying to separate fizz from cola.

"This is a family place. I like it for the variety," she explained.

"Don't you feel left out, a single woman in a family place?"

She shrugged. "It reminds me a bit of when I was a kid."

"So something was good about your childhood."

She gravely stared at him for a long moment. The temptation to tell him about her family grew. But she didn't look back, she didn't like remembering.

"How's Starlight?" she asked, floundering for a safe topic of conversation.

Dusty hesitated, then some of his tension fled. "Fine. I brought her home on Wednesday. Hank's been watching her. The pulled muscle has cleared up. You can ride her this weekend if you like."

"I would like." She couldn't help thinking about the injured horse, and the ride back to the ranch—doubled with Dusty. His arm now pressed hard against her back, like his chest had been last Saturday. His heat was mitigated by the climate control in the restaurant, but it still warmed her. She couldn't help looking at his strong thighs, stretched out before him as he sprawled leisurely in the chair. He casually studied the other patrons.

When their number was called, Dusty rose and went to get their pizza. Deb noticed the women seated by tables along his way glanced up, then took a second look. Sometimes a third. They straightened in their chairs, brushed hair back, smiled. Deb grinned, amused. Obviously the man attracted attention wherever he went, and not only from the females in the crowd. Some of the men, and a couple of the teenage boys studied him. Probably wanted to emulate him—cocky, assured, sexy.

She reached for napkins, trying to block the image that flashed into her mind.

"It looks good," he said, setting it in the center of the table.

"Do you eat much pizza at the ranch?" she asked.

"Sometimes Ivy makes it. But she doesn't like to. And we don't get delivery service because we're too far out."

"Why doesn't Ivy like to make pizza?" Deb asked, taking a bite.

"Because she has to make so many."

His finger wiped her chin, held up a strand of mozzarella. Embarrassed, Deb brought up a napkin and captured the cheese. Dusty leaned forward until he was just inches from her face.

"You have some sauce on your lip. Shall I get that, too?"

She wiped her mouth, her eyes catching with his. Heat burst through her as she imagined his tongue taking care of the sauce. Swallowing hard, she tried to break the spell. Mesmerized by his gaze, she could only look back helplessly and feel the growing awareness take over. Desire pulsed and Deb again wished they'd ordered in and not left the condo.

"Maybe pizza was not such a good idea," she said, her breath mingling with his.

"Maybe a cold shower would be a good idea," he said in a husky voice.

"Dusty."

"You know your problem, sweetcakes?" he said, sitting back and reaching for another slice of pizza.

"I'm sure you'll be happy to tell me." Scarcely able to get the words out, Deb took a deep breath and tried to calm her rioting senses.

"In the corporate world everything is made to look the way you want it. In my world, everything is the way it is."

"Is that so?"

"So I want you, that's the way it is."

"Dusty!"

"And you want me. But being from the corporate world, you have to hide that fact and pretend you're far above such mundane feelings."

Startled, Deb shook her head. "I admit I'm attracted to you. I just don't think I should act on that attraction."

"Why not? We're two consenting adults, no ties to anyone. We know it won't go beyond a brief fling."

"It sounds so cold," she said slowly.

"Honey, it would be anything but cold, I guarantee it."

Deb ate slowly. She was attracted to the man, more than to anyone she'd ever known. But he wasn't what she was looking for. She wanted stability and success. She wanted a man as different from her father as she could find, and Dusty was too similar—charming, carefree, live for the moment. Was this what her mother had faced? Had she found herself in love with a man who couldn't hold on to a dime? Had there been love before the anger and despair?

Dusty's finger came beneath her chin and he tilted her head up to his.

"Deb? It's all right to say no. I told you there are no strings on this weekend. Ivy would like to see you again, the boys enjoyed meeting you and talking with you at the barbecue. There's a barn dance at a neighbor's we could go to. Come and have a good time. We'll discuss our mutual attraction some other time."

"You drive me crazy," she said softly.

He smiled, "Is that so, Ms. Harrington? Well, you drive me there, as well, so maybe we'll meet up."

"But no dance. I'm not up to that." She hadn't the first clue about Western dance.

"Agreed."

"Tell me something about your ranch, Mr. Wilson." That should hold him awhile. Give her time to get her raging hormones under some sort of control before they got into the close confines of that truck of his and headed for the Wilson Ranch.

"Like what?"

"How long have you had it? Was it your father's?"

"No, it belonged to my father's brother, Samuel Wilson. He died a few years back, left it to me. He'd had two sons. One died as a child. My cousin Todd was killed in an automobile accident right out of college. Really hit my uncle hard. When he died, I was surprised to learn I was the beneficiary under his will. He knew me best of my dad's kids. Todd and I were the same age, hung around together when family got together."

"That's so sad," Deb said, thinking about families.

"It's hard when a child dies before the parent."

"Do you want kids?"

"Sure do, a houseful. That's one of the things Marjory and I fought over. She couldn't take time from her fast track to have children. I always thought one day she'd wake up and regret not having kids, but I don't know. Maybe her career is all she needs."

Deb licked her lips and remained silent. There was too much

similarity between Marjory and herself. And Dusty always seemed to home in on it.

"How long have you been divorced?" she asked. He'd told her once before, but she hadn't paid attention.

"Three years. Marjory took one look at the ranch and ran like hell."

Deb ate silently, thinking about Dusty and his ex-wife— wondering if Marjory had been as frustrated at his casual attitude toward everything. She must have suspected Dusty would let the ranch fail, and cut her losses before it happened.

Sighing, she reached for her beer again. She couldn't help it, she liked being around him. But she knew he wasn't for her. She had to focus on her career. No more fantasies about some rugged cowboy.

"Did you inherit Ivy and the others when you inherited the ranch?" she asked.

He nodded. "In a manner of speaking. Some of the men are new, but several worked for my uncle. And Ivy has done the cooking for the last seven years. I'm glad they held in there."

The song on the jukebox changed and Deb looked around. Everyone seemed to be enjoying their dinner. The parents at tables talked, laughed, and gently corrected rambunctious children. At a table near the front a young couple sat talking, heads close together. No children yet, she thought, but she bet they were newlyweds. A feeling of satisfaction seeped into her. She had wanted to share in this slice of life, and now she was here. And she had Dusty to thank for that. Not that she could tell him. But for the first time in a long time she felt as if she were a part of something, not just peeking in from the outside. It showed her how life could be. Maybe would be for her one day.

"Finished?" he asked.

Deb nodded. "Have that last piece."

He hesitated, then took it. She smiled and her toe tapped to the rhythm of the song. "This is fun," she murmured.

"Want to play some video games? There looks like a lull."

The teenagers had swarmed to a large round table where several piping hot pizzas were steaming.

"I never have," she said slowly.

"You'll never learn any younger." Dusty finished the last of the pizza, then poured the last of the beer into her mug. "I'm driving, you finish that. Come on, I'll spot you a few points."

"Sounds like a sucker play to me," she said, rising.

An hour later Dusty lost a game by six points. The teenage boys beside Deb cheered, while the girls hanging around Dusty moaned and complained. He shook his head, his eyes dancing in amusement and enjoyment.

Deb laughed at them and thanked the boys for their coaching. "Time to be going?" she asked.

He glanced at his watch, then nodded. "Good game." He held out his hand and when she shook it, hauled her close and kissed her. There were more good-natured cheers.

"Remember to anticipate," one boy said as they started to leave.

"I'll remember, thanks again," Deb called, waving. She had just spent the fastest hour of her life, and loved every moment of it. "That was great," she said as Dusty held the door open for her. The silence outside seemed magnified after the din of the pizza parlor.

"Who played who for a sucker?" he asked as they walked to his truck.

"I had never played. But when those boys came up to coach me, I had to do well. Couldn't let them down."

"Right."

"I noticed you gave your all for those girls."

"Trying to show them what a real man can do."

She giggled. "You just enjoyed their goo-goo eyes."

He laughed softly. "Yeah, well it's been years since any teenager thought to give me a second glance."

"I think you'll be their new idol."

"Great, just what I need."

She patted his arm. "Pretty soon they'll want autographs and photographs—"

"Next time we get a hamburger!" Reaching the truck, he opened the door for her.

Next time? she thought. Would there be "next times"? She hoped so.

"It's late," she murmured, checking her watch.

"Later than I thought to be leaving."

"Sorry, we shouldn't have played those games."

"Hey, I had fun and you did, too. No harm done. We'll just get to bed a little late, that's all."

"You must be tired, and it's a two-hour drive."

"I'm fine. How about you?"

"I'm fine, too."

But it would be after midnight by the time they reached the Wilson Ranch, and after late nights all week long, Deb was already fighting sleep as they made their way out of town. Darkness had long descended and she could only see where the headlight illuminated. Soon she felt her eyelids grow heavy.

When Deb slid against the door, Dusty looked over. She was fast asleep. His heart moved. He wanted to pull her against him and let her sleep until dawn. But he needed to drive. In the faint light of the dash, she looked younger than she was. Her hair was tousled, resting on her cheek. He watched as long as he could before he had to pay attention to driving.

He wondered what she'd been doing all week to make her so tired tonight. He should have given in to his urges to call her during the week, to talk to her, keep in touch. The need had been strong, but he'd suppressed it. Too often Deb reminded him of Marjory and he didn't want to get caught up with someone like that again. The hurt went too deep. But going in with his eyes open would make sure he didn't get caught. A few weekends together, a few nights in bed, he'd be ready to kiss her goodbye.

He thought of kisses. Deb inflamed him as no other woman had. He knew it had to be the result of abstinence. He hadn't made love to a woman in a long time. That's why she was so attractive to him, that's why he wanted her so strongly. Once they assuaged that yearning, he'd be able to back off and let her go. When it was time for family, he'd find a woman who put him and their family first, not one who demanded a fast-track career path.

Though, he had to be honest and admit, Deb seemed different from Marjory in several aspects. Marjory would never have gone to a pizza parlor to begin with, much less choose songs on the jukebox or play video games. And she would have had much better things to do than befriend teenagers, no matter how briefly.

He glanced over at Deb again, remembering her delight the first time she'd won a game. That damn corporate image had been forgotten. Deb had been a woman out for a good time. And he'd brought that about. Satisfaction settled. Maybe they'd share some more good times before her career interfered.

Dusty hated to wake her up when they arrived, so he stopped near the house and went to open the door. Returning to the truck, he eased open her door and caught her when she fell out, carrying her to her room. Gently he laid her on the bed and pulled off her shoes. He debated about the jeans, then decided to take the chance. They were too tight to sleep in comfortably.

Easing open the button, sliding down the zipper, his heart rate began to increase. Slowly he tugged and pulled until the denim slid down her legs. Shapely and long, his hand trailed over the silky skin as he eased the denim down. The service-able white cotton panties she wore were so practical and tied in with her view of life, he didn't expect to find them erotic. Swallowing hard, he dropped the jeans across the nightstand and yanked the sheet over her. Deb never moved. She'd probably never realize what a hardship it was to have him turn and walk away when he wanted to finish stripping her and climb into the bed with her.

"Good night, sweetcakes," he said softly, dropping a brief kiss on her lips.

It took a few moments when Deb awoke the next morning to realize where she was. She turned over in bed, and gazed around the room. Her small suitcase stood by the door. Her jeans were on the nightstand.

Her jeans were on the nightstand? Slowly she moved her legs, feeling the coolness of the sheets against her bare skin. She sat up abruptly. Shirt, bra, panties and socks all accounted for. But she didn't remember removing her jeans. If she'd begun to undress, she would have completed the task and put on her nightie.

Dusty banged on her door. "Deb, wake up!"

"I'm awake." And wondering just what went on last night, she thought.

"I'll wait for you in my office. Breakfast is in a half hour."

Twenty minutes later she paused at the doorway to his office. Dusty was sitting at his computer, tapping on the keyboard.

"Video games?" she asked, flustered when she thought of his removing her jeans. The bikini panties she wore were not much cover.

"Don't I wish. Actually I'm logging in some notes on the crossbreeding we're doing."

Wandering over to his desk, she kept a safe distance, yet curiosity was too rampant. Studying the screen, she realized he was using some sort of software program especially designed for breeding purposes. Somehow she hadn't expected this level of detail in his business. He'd seemed to have so many facts and figures in his head last weekend when he showed her over the ranch, she had assumed she carried everything in his head.

"Ready to eat?" he asked, shutting down the machine.

"Sure." Deb noticed the computer was the latest PC version, not inexpensive. She glanced around the office. The furniture looked old, well worn. There were no curtains or blinds on the windows, just glass that needed washing. But the view was spectacular. Maybe he didn't want window coverings because of the view. She wondered why he spent so much time outside when the house needed more work.

Even the bunkhouse was in better shape than the main house, she noticed as they swiftly crossed the yard. The early morning was frosty, her breath hung before her. Dark clouds boiled on the horizon and the air carried the hint of moisture.

"Hi, hon, glad to see you again." Ivy left the stove to give Deb a hug when they entered the warm kitchen. "Dusty said you'd be out this weekend. Though the weather looks like hell."

"A little rain never hurt anyone," Dusty said in protest.

"As long as it's rain and not snow," Hank said.

Dusty shrugged. "We've had a warm, dry fall, about time for it to change."

"Sit in your regular place," Ivy instructed Deb. "I've fixed a big breakfast today, being Saturday and all."

"We need it to keep up our strength," Hank said. "Especially if you plan to keep up with me at the dance tonight."

"None of your sass, mister," Ivy said, laughing.

Each of the men and women around the table welcomed Deb and in only a few moments, she was caught up in the conversation, asking what they'd done that week, what had happened on the ranch. For the second time in twenty-four hours, she felt a part of a group. It was totally unusual. It warmed her heart.

"What are your plans for the day?" Ivy asked as she finally sat next to Hank.

"I had thought to go riding," Deb said slowly.

"Not a good idea, today. Rain will be here before you know it. It should clear tomorrow and you can go riding then," Dusty said.

"Won't stop you from riding off," Ivy grunted.

"I've got work to do. I won't be gone all day."

"I've heard that before. Take a day off, entertain your guest."

"I don't need to be entertained," Deb said, a bit surprised that Dusty planned to do any work on the weekend. She would have thought he would jump at the chance to skip work to entertain her. Hadn't he invited her to visit? And from the looks of things, he wasn't a die-hard workaholic around the ranch. Was he up to something?

Ivy looked at Deb. "I could use some help. I'm planning on baking some pies."

Before Deb could reply, the men broke out with cheers and requests for berry or cream pies. It was obvious they were all crazy about Ivy's pies.

"Sure," Deb said when she could get a word in. She'd never baked pies, but Ivy could teach her. Tossing her head she glared at Dusty. She didn't need him to entertain her; she could take care of herself.

Dusty pushed back his chair and jerked his head. "Come with me," he said, turning to head for the back door.

Deb followed, wondering if anyone else noticed how quickly she jumped up.

The air was cool when he pulled the door shut.

"What?" she asked, watching him warily, leaning against the door.

He leaned close, resting on one arm near her head, almost encircling her with his body. His hand came up and brushed back the wisps of hair that stirred in the breeze. "If you need entertainment, sweetcakes, I'm your man, but later. I have some cattle to check this morning and if it rains, you'd just get cold and wet for no reason."

She drew in a shaky breath, his scent filled her nostrils. She didn't feel the slightest bit cold right now. Blood raced through her veins, and her skin tingled by just being near him.

"I didn't invite you out this weekend to ignore you, but I have to check the cattle first. Okay?" he asked coaxingly. His hand stopped playing with her hair, rested against her throat, his thumb gently caressing the throbbing pulse.

Deb couldn't have spoken if her life depended upon it. She swallowed, then nodded.

When the left side of his mouth rose in a lopsided smile, she thought her knees would give way and deposit her on the stoop like a puddle.

"Help Ivy this morning, and this afternoon, it's you and me."

Seven

"**Y**ou'll be all right with Ivy?" Dusty asked.

Deb nodded. "I believe so. Why, something I should know?"

He shook his head. "I wanted you to go riding with me, but the weather's going to be bad. Stay and bake pies. I'll be back as soon as I can."

"Don't get wet." She wanted to touch him, wished he'd kiss her. But he just smiled and opened the kitchen door.

"Any of you sorry cusses going with me today?" Dusty asked.

"Well, boss, payday was yesterday, don't want that money to burn a hole in our pockets, now do you?" Terry asked. "I need to head for town."

Deb listened to the gentle banter and tried to ignore her feeling of impropriety when the men teased their boss. She couldn't imagine kidding around with Mr. Montgomery. Was Dusty right? Did corporate life change people?

"Dusty's back," Ivy said, looking out the window some hours later.

Deb tried to control her heart rate, but it sped up despite her admonitions. "Is he?" She hoped she sounded casual. Hoped Ivy didn't have a clue how much she wanted to dash to the window to see for herself.

"Just rode into the barn." Ivy turned from washing the bowls they'd used, and smiled at Deb. "Might want to go over there and ask him if he wants something for lunch."

"Right away," Deb said, placing the last of the pies on the table to cool. She whipped off the apron Ivy had insisted she wear. Withdrawing a slicker from the hook near the back door she donned it for the dash across the yard. The rain had been steadily pouring since shortly after breakfast. But there was no danger from snow; it remained warmer than usual for early December in Colorado. Sometimes she found it hard to believe Christmas would soon be here. She wondered if Dusty decorated for the holidays.

Two minutes later she pushed back the hood and entered the cavernous structure. The barn felt warm and seemed redolent with scents of hay, grain and wet horse. She wrinkled her nose a bit and walked toward the back where Dusty stood, brushing water from his mount. He still wore a slicker, though he had opened the front.

"Hi," she said.

"Hey, sweetcakes. What's up?"

"Ivy wants to know if you want any lunch."

He drew in a deep breath, tossed the horse brush aside and reached for her. "You smell good enough to eat, like cinnamon and vanilla."

He didn't wait for her to agree or demur, he just leaned over and took a kiss. "How about I skip lunch and just have you?" he murmured against her lips.

"How about I bring you something to satisfy that appetite?" she whispered, never moving away from his touch, her lips moving against his as she spoke.

"My appetite isn't for food."

"Even apple pie?"

Dusty paused, pulled back and stared down into her eyes. "Warm from the oven?"

She giggled. "So much for desire. Apple pie wins every time."

He hugged her and rubbed his cold cheek against hers. "Only temporarily. Tell you what, you go get a pie and bring it out. Did Ivy get any ice cream?"

"Get a pie? A whole pie?"

"Sure, we'll share it. I like it best with ice cream."

"Dusty, we can't eat an entire pie." She searched his eyes to see if he was serious. He was.

"Why not?"

She paused, tried to think why not while his hands moved over her back, pressing her against him, tracing her spine, brushing the flare of her hips. Every inch became totally aware of the man. Deb had trouble thinking, she wanted to sink into a pool of sensation and enjoy.

"Sweetcakes, you haven't tasted anything until you've tasted Ivy's apple pies. Bring one out. If we can't eat it all, we'll take what's left back."

"And you think she'll let me waltz out of there with a whole pie?"

"No, you're going to have to sneak it. Don't forget ice cream." His hands moved to her shoulders and he gently shoved her toward the large double doors. "Hurry up. I'll finish with Diego here so we can eat when you get back."

Deb felt like a spy on a mission as she walked back to the bunkhouse through the rain. Somehow she had to get a pie and some ice cream out to the barn. And she could just hear Ivy on the subject. Maybe Dusty would be satisfied with a slice. She felt sure she could talk Ivy into a slice with a scoop of vanilla.

"I don't believe it! You have the most incredible luck, Dusty Wilson," Deb murmured when she walked into the empty kitchen. Listening, she heard nothing. Not questioning Ivy's disappearance, she darted to the freezer and found two containers of vanilla ice cream, one half empty. Scooping it up, she darted to the drawer she'd seen Ivy using earlier and snatched two forks and a knife. Then she headed for the pies. Footsteps sounded in another part of the building, drawing closer. Not waiting for plates, Deb grabbed the nearest pie, and headed for the door.

"I did it!" she exclaimed when she entered the barn. The rain had dampened the crust slightly, but she hadn't had time for a cover.

"Good girl, I knew you could do it."

"I didn't get plates, though."

Dusty turned Diego lose in his stall, and closed the half door. He shrugged out of his slicker and hung it on a hook.

"Don't need plates. Come on, let's eat. What did Ivy say?"

"She wasn't there," Deb admitted.

Dusty laughed, his eyes alight with amusement and delight as he looked beyond Deb. "She'll be on the warpath. Come on, up here." He took the pie, balancing it in one hand as he climbed up to the loft. Deb tucked the forks and knife into her slicker pocket and, holding the ice cream carton in one hand, followed.

Bale after bale of sweet-smelling hay stood stacked higher than Dusty's hat. He led the way toward the end of the loft, squeezed through a narrow gap and stopped when Deb followed. They were in a small enclosure, surrounded by hay and a partially opened door from the loft. The roof overhung the opening, sheltering it from the driving rain. She saw the large pulley and realized this must be how they hauled the bales into the loft. From the opening they had a clear view of the bunkhouse.

"Shh." He cautioned, his smile splitting his face.

The back door flew open and Ivy stormed out. "Dusty Wilson, you son of a gun!" she called as she headed for the barn, a slicker thrown over her shoulders.

"Where are you, you no-good wrangler? I'll skin you alive! Dusty!"

He laughed softly and watched Deb as her eyes widened.

"Dusty!"

"Shh," he said, placing a finger over Deb's lips as if he thought she'd speak.

"Deb, are you out here?" Ivy called.

Deb heard her stomping around on the lower level, then

heard her on the ladder. She sounded angry, but Deb couldn't help being caught up in Dusty's high spirits. She had never done anything like this. It was surprisingly fun. Surely Ivy wouldn't be truly angry.

"Dusty! No pie for you at dinner!"

Deb's gaze caught Dusty's as they shared the moment. In the distance, they heard Ivy mumble as she headed back toward the bunkhouse. A flicker caught Deb's eye and she watched as Ivy opened the back door to the kitchen and slammed it closed.

"We're bad," she said, giggling softly.

"So we get no pie for dinner. We'll probably make ourselves sick with this one anyway. But it'll be worth it. Open the ice cream."

Deb had never tasted pie so good. She had never shared an afternoon so enchanting. Dusty entertained her as they ate the pie, telling her of escapades he and his brothers shared growing up. Of the pranks they'd played on their parents.

It was wonderful, and so different from her own childhood, she listened, fascinated, to his every word. She wished she could have shared in some of those escapades. Though today's had been enough for her. She never did things like this.

"I should be feeling bad about this," Deb said as they finished the last of the pie. Piling the empty ice cream carton inside the pie plate with the forks, she shrugged out of her slicker and, using it as a pad, leaned back against a bale of hay. It proved surprisingly comfortable in the barn. "Ivy will be so mad with me."

"I'll tell her I did it."

Deb swung around. "You can't take the blame for something I did," she said.

He shrugged. "It's no big deal. I've done it before."

"That doesn't make it right."

"Taking the pie was my idea. I've had the pleasure of eating it *and* putting one over on Ivy. I don't mind her tirades. They're mostly for show, anyway."

"Still, I stole the pie."

He chuckled. "Sweetcakes, it's not as if it wasn't my pie to begin with."

"I don't know."

"I do. Lighten up, Deb. Tell you what, I'll take the rap for a kiss."

"What?"

"Give me a kiss, and I'll tell Ivy I took the pie and tied you up until I finished, so you couldn't turn me in."

She laughed. "Like she'll believe that?"

"Who cares, it's all a game."

Deb sobered immediately. "That's all everything is to you, isn't it, Dusty? A game?"

"Not everything. I want a kiss, Deb."

She debated, for about half a second. Scooting across the wooden loft, she leaned over him and touched her mouth to his. It was like touching lightning to the hay. His mouth was warm; he tasted of cinnamon and vanilla ice cream. But she had only a moment to think before his arms came around her and he pulled her across his lap. Snugly up against him, Deb gave free rein to the kiss that he'd wanted.

The soft patter of rain played a background melody. The air was fresh and crisp, but she felt warm pressed up against this hard cowboy's body. His arms pinned her against him, his hands moved, tracing the smooth sweep of her back, slipping beneath the waistband of her tight jeans, back up to her shoulders.

One hand brushed back her hair, then he plunged his fingers into the tangled mass and slanted her head at a different angle to deepen the kiss.

His tongue wreaked havoc with her equilibrium. When he traced her lips, she gave way to her clamoring senses and opened for him. Her hands tracked the strong muscles of his shoulders and moved up his neck to encounter his hat. Knocking it off, her fingers reveled in the thickness of his dark hair.

Gradually, Deb became aware of the hardness against her hip. Heat suffused her body. He had said he wanted her and, pressed against him, she had blatant proof. A sense of heady power filled her. This sexy cowboy wanted her!

Suddenly she felt as if her world spun around. Dusty scooted around on the floor of the loft and lay back, keeping her pressed against him until Deb lay half over him. Her breasts pressed against his chest, her legs tangling with his. Breaking the kiss, she raised her head and stared down at him. Taking a deep breath, the scent of rain and hay and man filled her nostrils. She licked her lips, tasted Dusty. She pushed against his shoulders and tried to sit up.

"Easy, sweetcakes. Just getting comfortable."

"Too comfortable. Let me up, Dusty."

"Hey, honey, relax. We're not going to do anything you don't want. You draw the limits here. We can share a few kisses, then head downstairs and face Ivy."

Hesitating for only a moment, Deb gave in to the rampant longings that crowded through her. Slowly she leaned back down. He met her halfway, his mouth already open for her.

Heat and cold, swirling rainbows and hard wooden floors, the sensations blended, mixed, faded in and out. Deb's only anchor in the world was Dusty, his arms tight around her, his mouth against hers, his heat keeping her warm. When he rolled them over until he lay on top of her, it felt right. Bales of hay towered over her, the open door gave way to the wild Colorado mountains and the steely, gray sky and the cool rain.

His mouth moved from hers to her cheeks, to her jaw, to her ear. Softly, gently, he bit her, then licked her lobe, continuing to soothe. He nipped her jaw, kissed it, tasted her with his tongue. Moving down her throat, he again paused at the pulse point, smiling against her skin as he noted the frantic beat.

His hands came up and rubbed her shoulders through her shirt. Down across her chest, her breast, to her waist. Back up again.

Deb moaned softly and shifted slightly to the left to give him better access. His hand caressed her again, then slowly began to pull her shirt from her jeans. Pushing it up, he rubbed his fingers against her bare stomach. Deb clenched with reaction, her eyes flying open to find Dusty's warm gaze.

"Feel good?" he asked, dropping a light kiss against her cheek.

She nodded, beyond words. It didn't just feel good, it felt wonderful, spectacular! Every cell focused on the shimmering waves of sensation pulsating from his fingertips. Slowly he traced his fingers across her abdomen, then even more slowly inched his way up across her ribs until the back of his fingers brushed the weight of her breast.

Deb held her breath, yearning for more. Yearning for his touch to assuage some of the ache in her breasts. Fiery heat threatened to consume her, yet she wanted more.

"Touch me," she whispered, staring up at him.

He smiled, and she felt as if she'd gone to heaven. How could she still be affected by his smile when they were doing so much more?

"I am touching you."

"All of me," she prompted.

His smiled widened. When his palm covered her breast, she gasped from the pleasure. Arching up into his hand, she closed her eyes to better concentrate on the sensations that coursed through her.

"Nice," Dusty murmured, pushing her shirt up to expose her breasts in their creamy, lacy bra. "Oo-ooh, sweetcakes," he said, fingering the lacy covering. Impatiently he rolled her slightly to reach behind her and unfasten her bra. Pushing it up, he stared at her, his fingertip lightly brushing over one pebbled nipple. "Honey, you are so pretty." He brushed the other nipple.

Deb thought she would die from the sensations that shot from each breast deep within her. She could feel the ache between her legs, feel herself grow damp. Still he didn't begin to satisfy. She arched again, wanting more than a tantalizing brush over her skin. She wanted—

Dusty lowered his head and kissed her breast, circling closer and closer to a thrusting nipple. Pleasure filled Deb as she drew in a deep breath and tried to commit every sensation to memory. She'd never done this before and wanted to remember every second.

When his mouth covered a nipple and sucked, she moaned and about exploded. Against her sensitized nipple, his tongue felt like soft velvet, stroking her, pressing her against the roof of his mouth, sucking gently, then harder.

She clasped his head to her, arching higher and higher. She was on fire, she wanted Dusty with a passion she hadn't known she possessed. While one hand threaded itself in his thick hair, the other tugged against his shirt.

He sat up suddenly. The cold air hit her wet nipple and caused it to tighten almost painfully. Deb drew a breath. Was he stopping?

But Dusty only yanked his shirt from his jeans and unbuttoned it. Flinging it open, he came back down on top of her, his hot skin heating hers. He licked the damp nipple, then moved to the other one. Pleasure swamped her. His mouth was so clever, driving her mindless with desire. She tracked her hands across the muscles of his back and moved beneath him. Her body burned, the fierce craving filled her and nearly drove her mad.

When his thigh pushed between hers, she spread her legs and arched up against him. Slowly she moved her hips, bucked against the rising pressure. She felt her jeans slacken when he slid her zipper down. The cool air hit her, but his warm fingers were there instantly to keep the cold at bay.

"Deb?" he asked, looking at her.

She opened her eyes. "What?"

"Are you sure?"

How could she be sure of anything with his fingers wreaking havoc on her soul? She could only feel and demand that the feelings never end. Wetting her lips, she opened her mouth to tell him she was sure. Catching a glimpse of movement from the corner of her eye, she turned her head—

Deb shrieked. She jerked against Dusty, pushing him away as she rolled to her knees and then stood, backing away, her eyes wide. Heart pounding, she stared at the bale of hay.

"What the hell was that about?" Dusty came to his feet and stalked over to her. Reaching out to grab her shoulders, he shook her slightly.

She looked at him, then around him, toward the corner of the loft.

"I saw a mouse," she said.

"Hell, is that all?" He dropped his hands and turned away in disgust.

"Is that all?" she demanded, still searching the hay for signs of the small gray creature. Shivering, she began to fasten her bra, then zip up her jeans. She wanted out of the barn!

"Field mice live in hay. Fact of life. I don't see any, though." Dusty turned back. His shirt hung from his shoulders down to his hips.

Deb eyed him as she pulled her shirt down and rammed it into her jeans. "You knew there were mice here? You were going to make love to me with mice running around?"

He shrugged and began to button his shirt. "I never gave it a thought. It's not like they are going to be romping all over us. They'll keep their distance. They're afraid of us."

"Right. Tell that to the one over there."

"I don't see anything."

"Well, I did. It was little and gray and had a long pink tail and came as close to me as you were."

"Not that close."

Before Deb could reply, the sound of horses and men talking wafted up through the open door. Dusty moved to the edge and peered out. "Well, thank goodness our mouse friend came when he did. Some of the men are back."

Deb picked up her slicker and put it on, pulling the hood over her hair. She knew she had hay stuck all over her, and she didn't want to have to meet the smirks of knowing cowboys when she left. Turning, she found the narrow wedge of space between the hay bales and hurried to the ladder. With any luck, she'd reach the bottom before they saw her.

She almost fell in her haste, but reached the ground by the time Hank and Terry rounded the opening to the barn. She smiled and headed out, her head held high.

"Deb." Hank nodded. Terry smiled and greeted her, as well.

"What are you doing out here?"

"Looking for Dusty. Maybe I should try the house." Without a backward look, she headed for the ranch house. Going straight to her room, she grabbed a fresh shirt and underwear and headed for the bathroom. Carefully locking the door, she turned on the shower. A few moments later she stood blissfully beneath the hot water, washing the bits and pieces of hay from her hair. And berating herself for her actions.

She couldn't believe she had let him touch her like that. But it was wonderful.

Well, maybe he did have a practiced hand. Weren't cowboys notorious for loving and leaving women? Or was that sailors? Never having known either before, she wasn't too sure. But it didn't matter. She had been mad. Utterly foolish. There was no future between a cowboy on the Wilson Ranch and a banker from Denver. No common ground—except maybe the strong awareness that arced between them each time they came close. But sex was not enough to build a lasting relationship.

A relationship? The last thing she wanted was a relationship. Or Dusty, either, for that matter.

She stayed in the shower until the water began to run cool. Maybe she should stay until it ran cold, she thought as her mind relived the moments in the hayloft. His mouth had been demanding and daring. His touch had been fire and ice. And she had loved every second.

But it was only physical attraction, she repeated over and over as she dressed. Well, maybe not totally physical. She liked listening to his stories, liked the delicious sense of naughtiness that manifested when she'd taken the pie. It was harmless, yet so different from her normal behavior that she felt like a wicked woman.

In fact, a lot about Dusty made her feel more alive than she ever had. Even arguing with him proved exhilarating. If only he could conform a bit more. Make more of himself. But the signs around the ranch showed he didn't care enough to keep things up. He seemed more the type to enjoy life and not sweat the small stuff—just like her father.

No, she would not start in on that. It had been her mother's mistake. She remembered her parents arguing, and how her mother constantly harped about her father's shortcomings. She had to have known them when they married so why had she tried so hard to change him? It would be an impossible task. Just as impossible for her to change anything about Dusty.

Not that she wanted to; he was charming enough as it was. But that didn't make him the man for her.

She dried her hair and pulled it back into a ponytail. Finally she opened the door, daring to venture forth, hoping she was prepared to see him.

The house was empty. She wandered back to the kitchen and looked out on the gray day. The barn was visible, but she couldn't see into the loft through the small door. Was Dusty still there? Or had he come down while Hank and Terry were taking care of their horses? What excuse would he offer? Maybe none, he was the boss. She brushed her fingers across her lips. He was also the best kisser she'd ever known.

Dusty listened as Hank and Terry talked while taking care of their horses. He sat on the loft floor and leaned against the hay, his eyes on the distant hills. Without Deb, he was getting cold. He rubbed his face with one hand. A lucky thing that mouse showed when it did. He would not embarrass her for anything, and having the men arrive just as they were—he shook his head. Maybe it wouldn't have to come to that, no matter how hot she felt in his arms. He wanted her more now than ever. She'd created a craving within him that only she could satisfy. He shook his head. He was heading for a major fall if he kept this up. She was too focused on her career to care about some cowboy. She wanted nice things, expensive things, material things. And he'd never cared much for things, preferring to be with people he liked rather than ones he had to impress.

So what was he doing bringing her here this weekend? And almost making love to her in the loft? In the loft of all places! She was probably at the house right now packing to get the hell out. Well, he wasn't ready to give up yet. And if she put up a fuss, he'd just deal with it. She had come for the weekend, and he'd make sure she stayed and gave him another chance to be friends.

Friends? He wanted more than that.

She was bright, had some wacko ideas about business being all-important, but beyond that, he liked being with her. She seemed to care about people. She'd been great with John, willing to help Ivy, asked about each of the men at the table this morning. And she was sexy as hell.

Besides, he wanted to make sure she didn't foreclose on John's ranch, didn't he? Better keep an eye on the lady until the situation was finally and firmly resolved.

When he saw Hank and Terry heading for the bunkhouse, Dusty rose and brushed down his jeans. He slapped his hat onto his head and picked up the pie plate. Slowly a smile lit his face. Deb was a co-conspirator in this. Maybe he could use that to his advantage.

Deb, staring out the kitchen window lost in daydreams, saw Dusty head for the house. She watched him draw closer, her heart pounding in her chest. She should leave. Should demand he take her home. Not because she was afraid he'd try to take up where they'd left off, but because she was afraid she would. She was afraid that she would be so locked into the man she would never want to leave. And that frightened her.

Dusty opened the kitchen door, surprised to see her. Crossing to the sink, he dumped in the pie plate and forks. There was no sign of the ice cream carton.

"Thought we'd better hide the evidence," he said.

Her lips twitched and for a moment she remembered the giddy excitement of taking the pie and running for the barn. "Is this like the purloined letter, we hide it in plain sight?"

He took off his slicker and tossed it over the back of a kitchen chair. "No, I thought maybe we could wash the plate and you could sneak it back into the cupboard. Then we'll pretend that Ivy miscounted the number of pies she baked." He grinned at her, his gaze roaming over her, taking in the change of clothes, the freshly washed hair.

She grimaced. "Oh, no, you don't. I'm not going to be caught smuggling in an empty plate. That would be tantamount to a full confession. Which, I may remind you, I don't have to make."

"That's right, I got my kiss." When his eyes looked into hers, she went still. Memory of the kiss flared between them. It had been much more than a kiss.

Nodding, Deb waited for him to speak.

"All right, you wash the plate while I take a quick shower. I'll smuggle it in."

"If you get caught, she'll skin you alive."

"A chance I'll have to take," he said with a heavy sigh.

Deb smiled and then looked away. "I should go home," she said.

"No, Deb. Don't go. I'll take you tomorrow afternoon like we planned. Stay for the weekend."

"I don't know."

He stepped closer, cautiously, as if approaching a skittish colt. "I'm not going to apologize for what happened in the barn. I enjoyed it and I thought you did. But I think maybe we're going too fast. We don't have to go so fast. We can take our time."

"But why? We aren't heading for a long term relationship, we both know that. You and I want different things from life."

"Do we, Deb? What do you want?"

"Stability and security," she said promptly.

"And a fancy address and sleek foreign car."

"I worked hard for the things I buy. I don't have to answer to anyone on how I spend my money."

"And that gives you security?"

"I happen to have a nice stock portfolio, as well, that's what gives me security. That, and knowing I'm good at my job."

"Hell, we're back to the almighty job now."

"You're back to it. It suits me fine."

"And ranching just doesn't offer the stability and security you're looking for, is that it, sweetcakes?" He almost snarled the words as frustration built in his eyes.

"Ranching is probably as stable as any other business these days," she said slowly. She turned to the sink and ran the water. Needing something to do, she'd wash the pan. Maybe

Dusty would let the inquisition drop and go take his shower. She shouldn't have started this, she should have stayed home.

His hand grasped her arm and swung her around. Reaching behind her, he shut off the water.

"This is just getting interesting. If it isn't ranching, then it must be the man."

She stared at the strong brown column of his throat. He was so darkly tanned from his hours in the sun. His chest was the same bronze color. She swallowed, remembering his chest against hers, his mouth on her. Shimmering waves of excitement snaked up her back. She couldn't give in to attraction, not if she wanted to be in charge of her life. She had to take control.

Bravely she met his gaze. "Sometimes I don't like you," she said.

"Could have fooled me in the barn."

"That's sex. I'm attracted to you, I admit that. But I don't have to do anything about it."

"Because you don't like me," he stated, releasing her and fisting his hands at his sides. "And why not? Because I threaten your secure little world?"

"Yes, you're a threat to what I want, what I'm determined to get. I won't fall in love with a man who can't make something of himself. I won't live my life like that." She'd seen too much misery to put herself in the same situation.

"Whoa, sweetcakes, hold up a minute. What's this bit about making something of myself? I own a ranch. I'd say that was doing all right."

"Dusty, it's falling down around you! The house needs to be repaired and painted. The corral looks like it's teetering on the verge of collapse. Your furniture is old and—"

"And it wouldn't do for anyone to see it. Right? I'm sure you have ideas on renovating the place."

"A bit of hard work wouldn't hurt," she snapped.

"A bit, sweetcakes, or unceasing—like you do? Day in and day out. Nights, too, right?"

"I do what it takes to get ahead. Instead of playing pie thief today, you could have been doing something. Painting the living room, or repairing the corral fence.''

He stood erect, his expression impassive. ''I was entertaining a guest. And if you will recall, I did go out this morning.'' He shook his head and looked at the ceiling for a moment. ''Damn, I can't believe I'm justifying myself to you.''

''You don't have to.''

''But let's get one thing cleared up. I don't want you to fall in love with me, I want you to sleep with me. There's a big difference. I'm not into happily-ever-after. I tried it once and it blew up in my face and I won't do it again. We talked about that before, Deb. We're both free and available—if we have a mutual itch, why not scratch it?''

''Oh, that's romantic.''

''Don't get romantic with me. Falling in love would be the worst thing you could do.''

''I didn't mean I was falling in love with you. I would never do that!'' Deb almost screamed the words.

''And why not?'' His voice was low, ominous. Anger shimmered around them. His glare could melt ice.

''You're too much like my father.''

Eight

"**Y**our father?" Whatever Dusty had been expecting, it wasn't this. Boiling with temper, he kept a tight lid on it. He wanted to throw something, preferably miss snooty banker herself, but he kept his hands fisted and refrained from moving.

"How do I remind you of your father?"

"He was like you—charming, cocky, handsome. He wanted to laugh more than he wanted to eat. But he could never settle at any one job. The future was always over the next hill. He'd get a line on a fantastic deal, but it required more work than he was willing to put in. He'd charm the socks off you explaining why there was no money—so it was pancakes for dinner again, because that's so cheap. He'd make it a game—why we had to move again when what it really boiled down to was that we were so far behind on rent. Wasn't it fun to camp out in the car for a few days? Or scoff at doctors? Using the line of distrust as a reason why we couldn't see the doctor unless we were almost dying. But all of it was because we had no money. He even joked when explaining why he couldn't keep his daughter in proper clothes. Being charming came easy to him. What didn't come easy was living with a man like that and trying to make it in the real world.''

Dusty looked at Deb, seeing a frightened child scared of the future because her father couldn't provide for her. No one should have to experience that. His own childhood had been safe and secure. Love was plentiful in his parents' house, as was money. He'd never gone without anything.

''I'm not like your father,'' he said evenly. If material things were so important—well, hell, of course they were to her. She had gone without for so long, no wonder they represented stability and security. The insight into her motivation for wanting expensive things didn't make it more palatable. People were a sight more important than fancy cars any day. But it helped to understand her.

''I think you are, Dusty. You're certainly charming enough for four of him.''

He wanted to be flattered she found him charming, but she hadn't meant it as a compliment. He could set her straight on a few things, but pride held his tongue. If she thought so little of him, she could head for home. And he could forget her. He'd be the world's biggest idiot if he got tangled up with some career-minded woman again. They were out for themselves first, last and foremost. He needed to recognize that, send the lady home and get on with life.

Except…he still wanted her. Angry color rose high in her cheeks, making her eyes all the more violet. She looked beautiful, and so alone. His heart cracked a little at her comments. Her explanation of the life she'd led as a child brought it all into focus.

''Your father is dead now, right?''

''He died when I was a senior in high school.''

''And your mother?''

''When I was nine. But I remember her. I remember the fights they had, the yelling and harsh words—all for lack of money. I remember the way they would call each other names and slam things.'' Involuntarily, Deb shivered. ''I hated the fights. I hate yelling and loud noises—even after all these years. And I still miss my mother.'' Dropping her gaze, she turned away, unable to believe she'd told him all that ancient history. Unable to believe she'd yelled at him. She hated confrontations like this. She wanted to run, to hide, to recapture the peace of her existence before this man had invaded her life.

Dusty glanced out the window. "It's getting late. Be time for supper soon. If you want to go back tonight, I'll take you. If you want to stay through tomorrow, the weather is supposed to clear. You could ride Starlight. Either way, it's your call."

Deb hesitated as the anger and fear began to fade. She shouldn't have said everything she'd said. Shouldn't have told Dusty about her parents. It wasn't anything but old history and meant nothing to anyone but herself. She looked at him, tried to determine if he meant anything beyond the simple invitation.

"I'd like to go riding again. If it's no trouble, I'll stay until tomorrow."

"Fine."

When he headed toward the hallway, Deb floundered for something to say. Something to ease the tension of the past few minutes. She shouldn't have attacked him so harshly, but maybe it would be better in the long run. At least they were both clear on where they stood.

"I'll wash the pie plate."

"Don't bother. I'll tell Ivy I took the pie. She works for me, she has nothing to say about the matter," he said.

She bit her lip, tears welling. She had destroyed something precious. The game was over. He sounded tired and distracted. Gone was the fun-loving camaraderie of the afternoon. She'd felt so carefree and young when they'd feasted on the stolen pie. Now the fun had shattered, and it was her fault.

She didn't want to change Dusty, just keep control of her own emotions. She dared not risk falling in love with a man like her father. She couldn't live that way. But she ached with longing and attraction for the sexy cowboy who lived in a rundown ranch. Whose easygoing ways were so different from hers.

Deb didn't know what Dusty said to Ivy when they went inside for dinner, but Ivy never mentioned the pie. Nor did she speak to Deb during dinner. Susan and Steve were planning to drive to the neighbor's for the dance and talked nonstop. Jessie and her husband were absent from dinner, gone for a weekend in Denver. Deb listened to the conversation that floated around her, conscious that Dusty rarely joined in. He smiled when appropriate, but the amusement didn't linger in his eyes like it used to. Guilt hung over her. He'd done nothing wrong, only been himself.

And that scared her.

When the meal ended, Dusty stood and cleared his place. "I've work to do in the office. Maybe Deb could stay here and watch TV with you." Without waiting for confirmation, he strode from the dining hall.

Deb blinked, feeling like an unwanted parcel. She glanced around the table, but no one else seemed to find much amiss, except Ivy. That woman's speculative gaze rested firmly on Deb.

"We're going to the dance. Guess Dusty forgot," she said.

"Come on. I'll set you up, Deb. We'll get the remote first and choose whatever we want," Terry said, pushing back his chair.

By the time Deb had had enough television, the rain had stopped. She declined an escort. There were only a few dozen yards separating the house from the bunkhouse; she was capable of crossing that distance alone. She hurried. The rain had left the air cool and fresh. Stars had broken through the clouds and the wind had died. The house was dark except for a window on the ground floor—Dusty's office.

Entering the house, she started for the foot of the stairs, then turned toward the light. Pausing in the doorway, she hesitated as she studied Dusty. She wasn't exactly sure what she wanted to say. But she didn't want to go to bed without speaking with him again.

He had his feet propped on the desk, a sheaf of papers in his lap. Whatever he was reading, it didn't please him; he wore a frown. From time to time, he'd make a notation in the margin.

"Dusty?"

He looked up, his scowl deepening.

"What?"

"I wanted to talk to you, if you have a minute?"

He let his feet drop to the floor, placed his pencil between the pages he was reading and dropped the papers onto the desk. "About what?"

"This afternoon. I'm sorry for the things I said. I had no right to say all that. I never meant to hurt your feelings or anything."

"Never thought you meant to. You just stated things as you see them."

"Is there any way to make it right again?"

He studied her standing in the doorway. "Why should we, Deb? You made your position clear. You don't even like me. Why would you want to make it right? You can ride Starlight tomorrow, I'll take you home in the afternoon. End of relationship."

"Maybe I don't want it to end," she said slowly.

"And maybe I should wait for you to make up your mind before deciding anything. You go home tomorrow and think about what you want in your life. If it includes me, give me a call some day and I'll let you know how I feel then." He glanced at the papers on the desk. "Is that all?"

"Yes." She turned and hurried to the stairs. Skipping every other one, she soon reached the second floor. Once safely behind the closed door to her bedroom, she rubbed her chest. The ache became almost intolerable. Why had she thought a few apologies would make up for her cruel words? She had no right to denigrate his lifestyle, point out the shortcomings of his ranch. She objected when he criticized her, she should know better than to criticize him.

And she had no experience for the devastation she felt now that he no longer seemed interested in her. Did she just want him pursuing? She couldn't be that shallow. It was more—she enjoyed being with Dusty. She liked his humor, enjoyed his touch, felt safe when around him. Was there any way to return to the carefree relationship they'd shared that afternoon? To the passion that had sprung up between them?

Undressing slowly, Deb tried to find a way out of the tangle she'd made of things.

The next morning Deb slept in late. No one woke her by a knock on the door. No one urged her to hurry so she wasn't late for breakfast. And she was late, very late.

When she arrived at the bunkhouse kitchen, Ivy was nowhere in sight. The lingering aroma of coffee, bacon and biscuits filled the air. But every plate and cup had been washed and put away.

She looked in the pantry, and brought out the last slice of pie. Taking a bite, she pushed it away. It reminded her of yesterday. She still hadn't come up with an idea on making things better—reminders of happier times were unwanted.

Grabbing a cup of coffee from the pot that Ivy kept going all day, Deb wandered around. Where was everyone? She entered the living room. The large-screen TV stood silent in the corner. No sounds came from the bedrooms that stretched out beyond the room. Had everyone left?

Finishing her coffee, she rinsed the cup and left it on the counter. Walking to the barn, she searched for someone, anyone.

"Hello?"

"Hello. Deb, is that you?" Terry came out of the tack room, a bridle dangling from his hands.

"Where is everyone?" she asked, grateful to find she was not alone on the ranch.

"Most of them went to church. Dusty and Hank and Steve are out checking some of the feeder dams after yesterday's rain. Bart and Jessie won't be home until late."

"Are you getting ready to go somewhere?" she asked, gesturing to the bridle.

"Yeah, thought I'd ride over to the Lancaster spread. I've got a girl there."

And she'd been left behind. Not that she could blame Dusty

after her tirade yesterday. But she didn't want to just hang around the ranch house until he came to take her home.

"Could you saddle Starlight for me? Dusty said I could ride her. Maybe I'll see a bit more of the ranch." She'd only ridden that one time. But the horse had been quite docile. She could manage again. And it beat kicking herself in an empty house.

Terry hesitated, but when Deb pressed, he agreed. They rode from the barn together a few minutes later.

"I go this way," Terry said when they reached the edge of the corral. "Dusty's working that way." He pointed toward the left. "And Barrett's spread is over yonder."

Deb nodded and waved. She felt daring riding the horse alone, but she had managed well last week. Starlight wasn't likely to bolt and run. Reining the horse in the direction Terry had pointed for Dusty, Deb started. After a few minutes, however, she changed her mind. She'd go over and talk to John Barrett again. Tell him again she planned to hold off on the foreclosure for a little longer. Reassure him he had a bit of time. On Monday she'd have to see to the papers, make sure she listed why she held off on the foreclosure. She didn't want Mr. Montgomery questioning her later and wondering about her motives. The repayment of the loan was what counted. She could justify her decision.

Two hours later, Deb pulled the horse to a stop and looked around her. She thought she knew the way, but the gate hadn't been exactly where she thought it should be. The rise near Barrett's house wasn't in sight, though she'd tried several. Now she was hopelessly lost. And to make thing worse, dark clouds crowded the sky. If it didn't rain, she'd be lucky. But she had no idea in which direction the ranch house lay. Nor how to get back to it.

"Great. This comes from trying to be someone you're not. You are not a cowboy. You are a banker. If you had stayed in Denver where you belonged, you'd be home now," she muttered, trying to figure out which direction to try.

She dismounted, holding the reins as she walked slowly toward the next hill. She needed to stretch her legs.

"As I see it, Starlight, we have two choices. Keep riding

and hope we come across someone who can steer us home, or stay here and hope someone comes looking for us.'' Neither idea appealed. With a sigh, Deb remounted.

By the time Deb checked her watch for the one hundredth time, it was almost five. It would be dark soon and she was hungry, tired and growing just a little afraid. She and Starlight had been away from the ranch for almost eight hours. And the one bite of pie she'd had that morning hadn't gone far.

"I hope we don't have to camp out,'' she murmured, watching the horse twitch her ears at the sound of Deb's voice. "I'm not much of an outdoors person, or maybe you've already guessed that.'' She had tried just sitting on Starlight, hoping the mare would head for home. Instead, Starlight had stood patiently until Deb urged her forward.

She'd tried following the fence line, but saw no one, and came across two gates, both of which looked familiar, most likely because they were the same kind of aluminum gate she'd seen last weekend. Obviously all the gates looked the same.

"If I owned this place, I'd leave maps at each gate,'' she mumbled, wishing she'd see someone. "Of course Dusty would probably say all his men know their way around so why bother with maps. But I don't have a clue where we are.''

"Dusty!'' She stood in the saddle and called his name. Waiting several seconds, she eased down. Her thighs were sore, her bottom tired of the saddle. But when she walked, she didn't cover as much ground. "Which might not be all bad if we're heading away from the homestead, right, girl?'' She patted the horse's neck and debated what to do. The awful sinking sensation in her middle reminded her of the lost feeling she'd had as a child. She had never known what to do then, either.

If she remained stuck out all night, she'd need more than her jacket. She'd have to find someplace out of the breeze. It was already cool, and would grow colder still once it was dark. She urged the horse up another hill. Pausing at the top, she scanned in every direction. Nothing looked familiar. Deb made ready to push on when she caught a glimpse of something in the far distance, to her right. Squinting to see better, Deb recognized a horse and rider!

"Yahoo!" She jerked Starlight's head around and kicked her. The mare hesitated for a moment, then broke into a lope. "Whoa," Deb called as she lost her balance. In two seconds she landed hard on the damp ground. Starlight stopped dead and looked around at her fallen rider.

"I guess I'm not up to fast riding yet," Deb said, standing and brushing off some of the dirt. Her hip hurt as she limped to the waiting horse. "Let's hope the rider is still coming, we'll ride to meet him, but at a more sedate pace."

Mounting, Deb looked in the distance. The rider had seen her and had changed his direction, heading straight for her, his horse flying across the range. Slowly she and Starlight moved to intercept.

"Deb! Glad I found you. We've been worried." Terry drew reins and pulled his horse to a stop. "What the devil are you doing out here? I thought you were going to join Dusty."

"Thank God, you found me, Terry. I've been lost."

The cowboy smiled as he drew near. "Figured that. Dusty was in a rare turnup when we realized you were gone and no one had gone with you. It's easy to get lost out here, and you've come a long way." As he talked, he unsheathed his rifle. Turning a bit, he fired three shots. Starlight jumped and sidestepped, but did not bolt. Deb clutched the saddle horn, relaxing only when she reluctantly became convinced the horse wouldn't dump her.

"Letting the others know I found you. Come on, it'll take a while to get you back to the ranch. You've traveled some distance."

They began to head back the way Terry had come.

"Others?" Deb asked.

"The whole place is out looking for you. Barrett's got his foreman and some men out, Lancasters have their hands out." In the distance three more shots were heard. Terry nodded. "They're letting everyone know you've been found."

"Sorry to be so much trouble. I thought I would just take a short ride and see some more of the ranch. Then I got turned around, and everything looked the same. I passed several gates, but never knew which one was the one we used to get to Barrett's ranch.''

''I shouldn't have let you go off alone. Dusty made that clear. But you're found now, so all's well.'' Terry didn't speak again and they rode in silence.

Finally, giving in to hunger, Deb asked, ''Do you have any food with you? I'm starving.''

''Some jerky.'' He reached behind him into his saddlebags and withdrew a pouch of beef jerky. He reached across the span between the horses and handed it to her.

She broke off a piece and began to chew. It wasn't much, but at least gave her the illusion of food. Glancing at Terry, she began to think about all the people out looking for her. She was embarrassed to have caused so much trouble. It was Sunday, most people wanted to rest on their day off, not search the hills for a lost tourist. And she bet Dusty was furious. She should have stayed at the house.

As if thoughts of the man conjured him up, she turned her head when she heard the pounding of hooves. Dusty rode toward them, hot and hard. His horse was lathered and breathing heavily when he reined in and turned to match his gait with hers.

''You all right?'' he asked. He looked at every inch, as if imprinting the sight of her on his brain.

She nodded. ''Sorry I got lost. I'd hoped to find the Circle B and talk to John again.''

''Do you have a clue where you are?'' he asked in exasperation.

She shook her head.

''Barrett's place is way over there.'' He pointed to his right. ''And if you'd kept going, you would've ended up in Wyoming. As far as I know, there's not a house between here and the border.''

He was seething. She bit her lip. Yesterday had been bad enough, she didn't need this today. Terry said nothing, just rode easily in his saddle. She shivered in the breeze that kicked up. Grateful she'd been found before dark, she wondered how far it was to the ranch.

"What's in your mouth?" Dusty asked, noting the shiver.

"Jerky. I'm hungry."

"Terry said you left before lunch. I guess you are hungry."

"Mmm. Didn't have any breakfast, either." Another shiver.

"Hungry and cold?"

"A little."

"Serves you right. Dammit, this isn't a stroll down one of Denver's main streets, Deb. You have to be prepared for things out here."

"You don't have to rub it in, Dusty. Obviously I'm a fool about ranches and how to survive on them. Once back in Denver, I'll never venture forth again."

"Let's move out. We can get back to the house quicker at a faster gait than this."

"No!" Panic touched her. Her eyes met Dusty's. "I fell off when I tried to go faster. I don't think my riding skill is up to it yet."

He maneuvered his horse closer and reached out. Grasping her by the waist, he hauled her onto his saddle. "Terry, take Starlight. I'll take Deb."

"Right, boss." He snared the mare's reins and urged his horse into a faster gait.

"I didn't mean to cause all this trouble," Deb said as Dusty settled her in front of him on Diego. His warmth enclosed her and her chill faded.

"I know you didn't. Hold on, we'll be home in less than an hour." He urged the big gelding into a lope and tightened his arms around Deb.

It reminded her of the ride back from John Barrett's. His thighs moved beneath hers as he controlled his horse. His arms surrounded her, giving the illusion of safety. She closed her eyes and leaned back against him, reveling in his strength. She regretted her foolish words of last night, had wished a million times today that she could take them back. She loved being encased in his embrace. Wished it was more than expediency that found her here. Wished she could mean something special to this man.

Dusty was special in a way no other man had ever been. She didn't want today to be the last time he saw her. She loved his lopsided smile, his teasing, his lighthearted view of life. He might never amount to much, might never have the drive she had to succeed, but then things had come easy to him and he didn't have the history she had.

They flew across the grassy field. Stopping only once to pass through a gate, they soon reached the homestead. Too soon for Deb. She could have ridden half the night in his arms. She'd been lucky to be found, and she knew Dusty was furious with her, but she didn't care about any of it. Enjoying the feel of his body moving against hers, of the wind in her hair, and the beauty of Colorado surrounding her, she was as close to heaven as she'd ever been.

More than a dozen people waited in the yard, saddled horses stretched out along the corral. Deb blinked and recognized Ivy, Susan and the ranch hands. There were several unfamiliar faces. Everyone turned toward them when they arrived.

"Safe, I see." Ivy strode out in front.

"Just lost," Dusty said. He handed Deb off, dismounted and tossed his reins to one of the men.

"We were worried about you, hon," Ivy said with a quick hug.

Deb smiled and nodded, afraid to speak. The lump in her throat was unexpected, but so was the kindness of these people—most of whom she didn't even know.

"Thank you for looking for me. I should have taken a map."

Laughter greeted her comment. One or two mentioned wishing there were maps when they'd first come.

Dusty took her hand, laced his fingers through hers, and led her toward the bunkhouse. "This lady's hungry. And tired, to boot. Thank you for helping. Come in and let's raid Ivy's kitchen."

Ivy led the way, no doubt to keep some sort of order in her domain. Before long hot dogs and hamburgers were being grilled on the huge industrial stove, and everyone chipped in to load the table. There were too many to sit at the table, so they ate buffet style, spilling into the living room.

Deb met and thanked everyone while she ate. She was touched by their kindness. More than one had indicated the search hadn't been a problem, that they were glad she was safe.

"Ready?" Dusty asked as she finished the last of the food on her plate.

Her heart sank. Time to go home. Past time. They wouldn't reach Denver until late. And Dusty still had the return drive. Panic touched. She didn't want to say goodbye. Wishing desperately that each passing minute would slow down, she nodded.

"Yes, just let me get my things. Thanks, Ivy. The meal was great."

"Anything would taste good after a day without eating, hon," Ivy said.

"But not that good. Your cooking is special! Bye."

Deb said her farewells to the others and then followed Dusty to the house, her heart banging against her chest. She hated this. Wished she'd never met the man, never fallen—

"You're limping."

"I landed on my hip when I fell. It's sore. Of course, I'm sore all over. I'm not used to a day on the back of a horse."

"You need a hot bath, that'll take some of the ache away."

"We have to get to Denver."

"No rush, why don't you take tomorrow off and rest?"

"I can't. I have a meeting tomorrow morning."

"And would it kill you to skip one day, one meeting?" he asked.

"It's unprofessional. I've worked too hard on my project to let a little thing like this keep me from work." *Like some people would* dangled in the silence between them.

"Guess I'm not the best person to advise you on taking time off, huh?" Dusty said as they reached the front door.

"I appreciate the suggestion, but I'll be all right."

"Take a warm bath, relax your muscles. Then I'll take you home."

"Dusty, it's already late. If I bathe now, it'll be far later before you drop me off and head home."

"So stay the night. We'll get up early and I'll get you to work in plenty of time for your meeting."

His offer tempted. She would love to crawl into bed and sleep for hours. And the thought of a hot bath tantalized. Add to that the fact that Dusty normally rose early, and it would be better to make the trip after a good night's sleep.

"All right." Wanting to stay a bit longer had nothing to do with her decision. It simply made good sense.

The water felt heavenly. Filling the tub almost to the rim with hot water, Deb sank to her chin. Tiredness soaked away, a pleasant lethargy engulfed her. Now that she felt safe, she could view her day with a bit of pride. She'd seen a lot of the ranch, and stayed on her horse. Except for that one time. Drifting in a half-awake state, she daydreamed about Dusty. She wished he'd been the one to find her. Had they been alone, would he have kissed her?

She brushed her lips with her wet fingers, imagined how his mouth would feel. Would he have been rough with urgency, or gentle with love? Blinking, she shook her head, water flew from the wet ends of her hair. Much as she might want them, there'd be no more kisses. Dusty had made that pretty plain. But she had memories to warm her. Even the water seemed cool in comparison.

"Deb? Don't fall asleep in there." Dusty knocked on the door.

She smiled and let her eyes drift closed. No, she wouldn't fall asleep, not just yet. She didn't want to miss another minute of her visit. Time enough to sleep once she reached home. For now, all she had was fleeting time with Dusty Wilson. The last thing she wanted to do was sleep.

"Deb?"

The door opened and she felt cool air wash into the steamy bathroom.

"Deb, are you asleep?"

Raising her lids, she gazed into Dusty's hot blue eyes.

"No." Slowly she rose until she stood in the cooling tub, water streaming off her warm skin. "Could you hand me a towel, please?"

He swallowed, his eyes skimming over her.

"I'm getting cold with the door open," she lied. Flames licked though her as his eyes brushed over every inch of her. She wanted to fling herself into his arms and beg him to touch where he'd looked, to kiss her everywhere and hold her and never let go.

Her heart skidded then raced. Her breathing became difficult and she opened her mouth a bit to help.

"God, sweetcakes, you're beautiful." He drew a towel from the counter and opened it, wrapping her in it and lifting her from the tub.

His mouth found hers and Deb was consumed. She had come home. After her tirade, she'd been afraid he'd never kiss her again. That fear faded as she gave herself up to his embrace.

He kissed her mouth, her cheek, her neck, her shoulder. Brushing his lips against her skin, he found her mouth again, opening it wide and thrusting his tongue inside to sweep against hers. His hands moved over her back, slick with water, learning every inch of her. The towel slipped, but he refused to release her.

"Deb, I want you."

She shivered and tightened her arms around his neck, reveling in the fiery sensations he caused. He still wanted her! And she wanted him. If it were the last time they were together, they had better make the most of it.

"We have tonight," she whispered, her heart pounding in anticipation. She wanted him like she'd never wanted anything else. She was very afraid her defenses had been breached and she'd fallen in love with this carefree, careless man.

"Say it, say it right out loud so there's no misunderstandings," he said, pulling back a bit and looking down into her eyes.

For a moment she thought he'd read her mind, then realized

all he wanted to hear. "I want you, Dusty," she said clearly, her hands in his hair, her body pressed against his as tightly as she could make it.

"Even if I'm a charming, cocky, arrogant, good-timing, no-good cowboy?"

Pain squeezed her heart. She'd hurt him. She hadn't meant to, but she had.

Nodding slowly, she pressed her lips against his. "I want you, Dusty. If I could take back the words, I would. I'm sorry. But I still want you. If you want revenge, turn me down."

"I may not be what you want in a man, sweetcakes, but I'm not stupid. If I was after revenge, I'd find it another way." He swung her up into his arms and headed for his bedroom.

Setting her on her feet beside his bed, he began to yank open the buttons on his shirt.

"You're going to rip—" she began. Just then two buttons popped off and pinged across the room.

She leaned over and kissed his chest, growing shier each moment. Reaching out, she pulled back the covers on the bed and sat on the edge. He sat beside her and tugged off his boots. "Damn things take forever to get off."

She laughed and kissed his bare shoulder. Trailing her fingers across his biceps, across his muscular chest, she touched a flat brown nipple.

He groaned and pulled off a boot. Tossing it across the room, he turned and tumbled her back against the mattress, kissing her hard.

"If you don't keep your hands to yourself for another couple of minutes, we'll end up under the covers with my boot still on," he growled, kissing his way across her shoulder and over the swell of one breast. He paused, looking at her from beneath his lashes.

Slowly, his gaze capturing hers, his tongue licked the pink tip.

Deb trembled under the onslaught of emotions and caught her lower lip between her teeth.

Dusty finished undressing while she watched him, her body

singing with passion. When he was as bare as she, he lay beside her and gathered her into his arms.

"Okay, sweetcakes, you're sure about this?"

"I'm so very sure, Dusty." It might only be for the one night, but she'd have one night to remember forever. She knew better than to try to change a man. He was too far along to change. Her mother had never changed her father. But for tonight, she would forget they had no future, and give herself to the man she loved.

Lightly his hands ran over her body, from back to front, from shoulder to knee. The hard calluses on his palms tantalized and aroused as nothing else could. They were strong, hardworking hands. For a moment Deb wanted to think. Wanted to decipher the vague thoughts that flitted through her mind. But she became lost to the wonder of his touch and any thinking would have to be done later. Much later. For now she only wanted to feel, and glory in those feelings.

"Is your hip all right?" he asked as his fingers climbed from her hip to the soft underside of one breast.

"Fine. The bath helped." Even if it had not, she would not have told him. She would do nothing to stop the pleasure.

"Good." Dusty caressed her, fondled her. His hands molded her breasts, his mouth dropped kisses. When his tongue wet her, she shivered. He blew on her pert nipple, seemingly mesmerized by her reactions. When he took the pink point into his mouth, Deb arched as shafts of desire plunged through her. She moved against him, her hands learning every inch of his hard body. The muscles in his back moved beneath her hands as he did delicious things to her. She rubbed against his chest, drawing her nails lightly across one nipple. Satisfied with the result, she tried the other. His gasp of pleasure fueled her own desire until she couldn't tell where her pleasure and his began or ended. They were united.

Perspiration sheened her skin. She could scarcely breathe, yet never wanted to stop. "Dusty, I'm so hot, I'm burning up," she said as he laved the other nipple.

"Let's see if we can make you a bit hotter," he said against her stomach, his hands caressing her thighs. "Open for me, Deb. Let me see if you're ready."

She spread her legs as his hand cupped her. Shimmering waves of pleasure coursed through her. Moving her hips, she tried to ease the growing tension. She felt as if she would explode.

"Oh, baby, you're ready." Using his knees, he spread her legs wider, slipped between her thighs and cradled her head in his hands. Slowly he pushed into her.

Deb smiled at the sensation, stretching, filling, just a twinge of pain, quickly lost in the simmering heat that consumed her. She couldn't hold still, however, and moved against the waves that began to build.

"Slow down, Deb, slow down." He reached down and held her hips still. But still the pulsating tension deep within her built.

"I can't," she said, squirming against his weight, seeking, searching.

"I want it to last all night," he said, thrusting slowly in, pulling out, then thrusting again.

But the conflagration had begun, and couldn't be contained. Deb moved and Dusty moved with her, until they were both caught in the splendor that flung them high as the stars.

Nine

He was in one hell of a tangle. Dusty kissed her, his breathing gradually slowing. She tasted like ambrosia. He traced his tongue along her jaw, wondering if he lived to be a thousand if he'd ever tire of her.

Hell, who was he kidding? They were not going to be together if he lived to be a thousand. She didn't like what he represented. And she was worse than Marjory, if that were possible. At least Marjory hadn't thought him a no-account cowboy. Dammit, how could Deb think that? Didn't she have any eyes?

"Dusty," she said, kissing his throat.

"Mmm?" He must be heavy lying across her like this, but she felt so good he didn't want to move.

"Don't ever change," she said softly, tightening her arms around him.

"Huh?" He pushed himself up onto his elbows and stared down at her. She was so pretty. Her hair splayed all over his pillow, the ends still dripping from her bath. Her skin was flushed and soft, as soft as a foal's. Her eyes sparkled in the dim light and her lips were rosy and swollen. He licked them, wanting to crush her beneath him and begin again.

"I love you just the way you are, Dusty. I know we don't match and can't have any kind of future, but I didn't mean all the things I said the other day."

"Sure sounded like it to me," he muttered. What was that she said about love?

"I was upset. You remind me of my father, but that's all right. You're not my father. I'm grown now and don't need a father. I'd like it if we would at least be friends."

"Love is something you mention with friends?" he said, wanting things clarified. None of this mumbo jumbo that business people liked to dazzle ordinary men with.

She nodded, her eyes wide.

He didn't like the disappointment that pierced. Of course she didn't love him, she barely liked him. And because he was charming! Jeez, he didn't think he'd ever understand women.

Slowly he rolled over and brought her with him. Snuggling beneath the covers, he held her as she drifted off to sleep.

"What am I going to do with you, Deb?" he whispered. "Let you go, I guess. It's all I can do. Your life is too different from mine. But, sweetcakes, it's been great knowing you." As he drifted to sleep, he tried to figure out a way to keep their relationship alive, to see if they could come up with some compromise somewhere that could keep them going for a little while at least.

Deb awoke in the night, held against a hot male body. She smiled, every second of their lovemaking imprinted on her mind forever. Tracing her fingertips over the hard muscles of his chest, she memorized every inch. Slowly, so as not to wake him, she leaned over and kissed him, letting her tongue skim across his skin, reveling in the slightly salty taste. She breathed in their mingled scents and her heart tripped faster.

"Don't waste them, sweetcakes," a sleepy voice said.

"I didn't want to wake you."

"Any time you want to wake me this way, feel free." His

hand moved in a reciprocating gesture. It was like a match to tinder.

"Can we make love again?" she asked, already moving against the shivering sensations that began to build at his touch.

"If you're up to it, I'm up to it." He took her hand and put it against that part of him that stood ready. Slowly she encircled the hard, hot shaft, her fingertips lightly tracing the velvety skin.

They moved slowly, hands caressing, lingering. Their lips touched every inch, their tongues tasted. Soft words, sweet words were spoken in hushed voices. The darkness cocooned them, turned their world into a small place, with only the two of them.

As desire grew, Deb became more demanding. She wanted to feel him against her, in her. Wanted to have him as inflamed as she felt. Her hands moved faster, a bit rougher. He responded in kind until they were beyond soft words and gentle touches. Hard-driven cravings pushed them together and the fiery impact grew hotter and hotter until the explosion burned away the last of their gentleness and they moved together in a rampage that catapulted them over the top.

Slowly the embers faded, breathing resumed normal cadence and sated bodies relaxed into sleep.

"Deb?"

She struggled against that voice. She didn't want to wake up.

"Come on, Deb. Time to get going. You need to get home to change for work."

Work! Deb opened her eyes. It was dark outside, but the hall light illuminated the bedroom. She lay in Dusty's large bed, covered and warm, but alone. Rolling over, she saw him leaning over her. He was already dressed.

"Get up, sweetcakes. You have time for a quick shower, that's all. We need to leave in a half hour."

"I'll be ready."

He smiled and straightened. "I knew I could count on that."

There was no good-morning kiss, no love talk from the night before. Dusty was pure business. Which should have suited her, Deb thought twenty minutes later as they headed toward the lightening sky and Denver. At least there were no awkward moments, no trying to make things come right in the light of day. He said he'd take her home, and so they were on their way.

She had not gotten a good last look at the ranch, it was too dark. But she would remember it. She didn't need to see it again to know where the house stood in relation to the bunkhouse, or the barn. She didn't need to see the hayloft door to remember eating stolen pie, nor to see Starlight to remember her venture into riding. As a child she would have given anything to ride a horse. Funny how it didn't mean as much as she had thought it would.

She wished she knew what Dusty was thinking. Was he glad to get rid of her? Or would he think about her in the future? Once John Barrett's loan stabilized, they would have no reason to keep in touch. Unless he wanted to keep in touch.

The drive took two hours; Deb thought it felt like two minutes. When Dusty pulled up in front of her condo, he made no effort to get out of the truck.

"Plenty of time to get dressed and get to work," he said.

"Thank you for having me out this weekend," she replied primly, her heart raging. She didn't want to leave the truck.

"Goodbye, Deb," he said.

She stared at him, trying to pin a smile on her face. For years she'd had practice hiding her feelings behind the facade necessary to get ahead in business. She could do it one more time. "Goodbye, Dusty."

Her head held high, she climbed from the truck and walked into her home. He could not tell from her back that tears coursed down her cheeks.

Monday seemed endless. The meeting she'd hurried home for had been postponed. Her hip ached from her fall, and her disposition was fierce. She even snapped at Annalise. Fortunately, her secretary just grinned and commented, "I told you that cowboy would be trouble with a capital T!"

Tuesday when Deb arrived, she found Phil snooping around her files. Demanding to know what he thought he was doing, she was not put off by his smirk, but with nothing concrete, she shook her head and told him to ask her if he needed something from her files.

By Wednesday, Deb was ready to give in and drive out to Dusty's ranch. She couldn't stop thinking about the man. She had gone over all the reasons why she should not be attracted, but even saying the words out loud did nothing to diminish her longing to see him, to speak to him. To have him hold her and make love. She would forget the plans of a lifetime if he'd just consent to be friends.

Not friends. She wanted more. Maybe things could work. She spent the better part of the afternoon trying to devise ways she could work in Denver and live on the ranch. Or maybe they could find a ranch closer to Denver and Dusty could play cowboy on that one. Or maybe the bank would open a branch in one of the small towns that surrounded the Wilson Ranch.

"And maybe pigs will fly!" Deb ended, flinging her pencil across the room and scrunching up her notepaper. She was on company time, and the bank didn't pay her to daydream her life away. Time to get on with her life. On the way home from work, she'd stop by that lot near her place and get a Christmas tree. Decorating it tonight would take her mind off a certain cowboy!

Deb had half a mind to ignore the phone when it rang that evening. The lights were on her tree and she had carefully placed some fragile ornaments. Sighing, she answered it, ready to tell the salesman on the other end she was not interested.

"Deb?"

"Dusty?" She sat, her knees suddenly weak. She hadn't expected to hear from him.

"Yeah. I called to see how you were doing, after getting lost on Sunday, and falling off Starlight, and all."

"I'm fine. Well, actually, my hip is a lovely color of black and blue, but the limp makes for an interesting conversation starter."

"Did you see a doctor?" She could hear his concern over the phone wires.

"No, it'll be fine, Dusty. And I'm teasing about the limp. I make sure I walk correctly at work, no sense starting rumors."

"Right."

The concern vanished. The clipped word showed her that. Sighing, she took a breath.

"I take it Starlight is all right. No bad effects after riding all over creation for a day. You did say she was old."

"A meandering wander around the ranch isn't going to lay her up. She's fine."

"How're the others, Ivy, Hank, Steve, Susan..." Her voice trailed off.

"Do you really want to know?" His low sexy tone caressed her.

"I really want to know how you are," she said breathlessly.

"I miss you."

"I miss you, too. I was afraid your goodbye on Monday was final."

"I wanted it to be. But there's something about you, sweetcakes, that grabs a man and doesn't turn loose."

"I thought I wasn't your type."

"You're not, any more than I'm your type."

She cleared her throat. "I explained the other night, Dusty, I don't think you should change a thing about yourself."

"So it's all right if I go along as a no-account cowboy for life."

"I don't think that. Not exactly," she added honestly.

"What do you think, exactly?"

"Dusty, I don't want to fight on the phone. I'm glad you called me. I've thought about you a lot. We had fun together. I don't have much fun in my life, it's been so dedicated to work."

"Yeah, well, all work and no play can make Jill a pretty dull person."

She bit her lower lip. Did he think she was dull? Of course, she wasn't into flirting like the others at the barbecue had done so easily. She felt awkward around people, only comfortable when she was working with numbers and knew she understood all the rules.

"Hell." His voice came across soft. "Deb, I don't think *you're* dull. It's just an old expression."

"I know. But I don't do much besides work. I need the structure and security—"

"I know you do, sweetcakes. But you have security now in your job. Take a chance, venture out a bit. There's a wide world out there, Deb. Not everyone is out to get you, to snatch away your security. You've proven you can take care of yourself, now enjoy it a bit."

"I enjoyed last weekend, most of it, anyway."

"Which part did you like best?"

Making love with you.

"Eating pie?"

He chuckled. "Anything else?"

"Mmm, riding Starlight, until I realized I was lost."

"And?"

"Mmm."

"Deb, if you were here, I'd wring your neck."

"Okay, maybe I enjoyed Sunday night."

"Maybe?" The growl on the other end sounded ferocious.

She giggled. "Yes, I loved Sunday night. I would love to make love with you again. There, are you satisfied?" Heat flushed her cheeks. For heaven's sake, she was almost thirty years old, alone in her condo, and she blushed because she admitted she wanted to make love with the man she loved.

"Hell, no. I'm on the ranch, you're two hours away in Denver and you tell me you want to make love again. You think that satisfies me?" He almost shouted.

Deb winced, then smiled. He was teasing her; the loud voice wasn't wounding. She could tolerate this. "So maybe you would like to come visit me this weekend?"

"I guess I could. Can you pencil me into your busy schedule?"

Ignoring his sly comment, she began to look forward to the weekend. "We could see a show, go eat—"

"I want to go dancing. Know a place where we can go dancing?"

"I'm not much of a dancer."

"Anyone can slow dance."

"Annalise will know a place. I'll check with her tomorrow. Come Friday and stay until Monday."

"Whew, sweetcakes, you're asking a lot of this ole cowboy. Stay in the big bad city for all that time?"

"I think you'll live."

"Especially if you're offering room and board."

"I am." The heat washed up again.

"Then count on me, Deb. See you Friday."

Count on him. She wished she could.

"Well, something put the sparkle back into your eyes," Annalise said smugly the next morning when she greeted Deb.

Not bothering to deny it, Deb nodded happily. "I need to get a recommendation for a good place to go dancing."

"Dancing?" Annalise swung from behind her desk and herded her boss into her office, closing the door behind them. "I need information. Who is going dancing, and when? Is this the Lone Ranger that was here a couple of weeks ago?"

Deb nodded, color staining her cheeks. "We've been seeing each other, casually, of course." No sense letting her assistant know how desperately in love with Dusty she was. She was plain lucky he planned to come this weekend. She refused to dare to dream—things could end at any moment.

"Of course. So you want to go dancing. Now I know a dozen places, but I need to know what you're looking for. Slow and dreamy?" Annalise asked slyly.

"I guess." The thought of being held in Dusty's arms while they slowly moved to seductive music appealed immensely. "Yes, slow and seductive."

"Whoa, seductive yet. I think there's more than meets the eye, here, Deb. Give."

"If and when there's anything to report, I'll do so. But I do want a good place to go."

"And something new to wear."

"I don't think—"

"Don't think, just buy something. Do you have anything dreamy in your wardrobe, or is everything business suits?"

"I have jeans," she mumbled, shoving her purse into her lower desk drawer and sitting.

"Go to Augusta's in the Sixteenth Street Mall. They have the best clothes and you're guaranteed to find something perfect."

"Maybe at lunch."

"No maybe, do it. I can go with you, if you like," Annalise offered.

Deb hesitated only a moment before agreeing. They arranged a time and finally got to work.

Deb's attention split between the various tasks she had to accomplish before the end of work the next day, and anticipation about Dusty's impending visit. She would have to clean the condo tonight, get some food in for breakfasts and lunch. At least the tree was up. Maybe she should bake some Christmas cookies. They could eat out for dinner. She wasn't crazy about cooking, baking was different. The list grew as the morning progressed.

Shopping with Annalise proved exciting. Her assistant had her try on a dozen different dresses, critically analyzing each one for their best features, finally indicating that Deb could choose between two, the deep blue and the soft white. Unable to make up her mind, Deb splurged and bought both, surprising herself and Annalise.

She had never had so much fun shopping and made a mental note to ask Annalise again, on a weekend when they'd have more time. While they had looked over accessories, Deb saw the perfect set of earrings she'd get her secretary for Christmas.

The dresses hung on the back of her office door during the afternoon, encased in the white bags from the boutique. She peeked at them from time to time, almost giddy with excitement. She hoped Dusty would find them pretty on her. She felt so elegant twirling around in the dressing room. She'd try them on again when she got home.

By midafternoon Deb counted the minutes until she could call it a day. She tried reading a prospectus for a new development that wanted financing. The project looked good, solid backers, and an excellent location—

The loud slamming of her door was the first indication of disaster. Deb jumped as if she'd been shot, adrenaline pouring through her system as she looked into Dusty's blazing eyes.

"You conniving, lying witch!" He threw a handful of papers on her desk. They skidded across the surface, fanned out. Two landed in her lap.

"Dusty? What in the world—"

"Don't even talk to me. I believed you. I trusted you, despite my better sense. You make Scrooge look like a saint!" He pounded her desk with a fist, his eyes almost shooting fire.

"I don't know what you're talking about." The yelling almost paralyzed her. She could hear her father attacking her mother. She tried to breathe, but she was caught up in fear and it proved difficult. The room spun around, she tried to make sense, but panic reared up and threatened to swamp her.

"I'm talking about your foreclosing on John Barrett. About stringing me along, keeping me off your back while you sneaked around to do your duty to your glorious bank. Hell, you didn't have to sleep with me to throw me off the track. That seems a bit extreme."

"I didn't!" Deb rose, instantly aware she didn't have her shoes on. She stood inches shorter than she wanted to be, inches shorter than the irate man standing in front her. "I didn't go behind your back. I didn't foreclose on John. We are holding—"

He shook his head. "It won't wash anymore, *Ms*. Harrington. The papers were served this morning. I've already spoken with your boss. He's unwilling to do anything to change things. But he got an earful of how his up-and-coming executive officer lies and cheats and stalls behind people's backs.

If that's the way he wants to do business, you two deserve each other!''

Panic built. Deb gripped the desk. "Dusty, slow down. I don't know what you're talking about.'' She picked up the papers, but could scarcely read them. Her fingers trembled, her whole body shook. She hated loud words, slamming doors. She couldn't think, lost in the flashback from the past.

"In addition to talking with your boss, I paid John's debt in full. The foreclosure will be canceled. In the future if John needs any more loans, he can find another bank. Since the matter is closed, there's no need to string me along. Goodbye, Ms. Harrington, I hope you rot in your glorious job!''

Turning, Dusty strode across the room and flung open the door so hard it jarred against the inside wall. The dresses bounced off the hook and slid to a puddle on the carpet.

Deb stared at his retreating figure, unable to move, to speak. Her heart pounded so hard in fear that she could scarcely breathe. Holding on to her desk, she felt shell-shocked. Something was wrong, hugely wrong, but she couldn't even think.

"Deb." Annalise appeared in the doorway, her face echoing Deb's shock. "Mr. Montgomery wants to see you right away. He's called twice. He sounds furious."

Deb pulled into her driveway and sat, too dispirited to even get out of the car. She stared at the mock Tudor lines to the condo complex, at the manicured lawns, the sculptured shrubbery. Her neighbors had strung Christmas lights and hung a holly wreath on the door. The complex looked pristine fresh. Just the opposite of how she felt.

Taking her dresses, she walked to her front door and opened it. She tossed the two bags across the back of the sofa, glanced at her tree and almost groaned. She'd been so excited last night after his call. Deb rummaged around in the cupboards. She wasn't much of a drinker but needed something. When she found some brandy, she wrinkled her nose, and poured herself a hefty tumbler. Returning to the living room, she crossed to the window to look out. In the distance, the tips of the snow-capped Rockies were visible. But the spectacular view provided scant comfort tonight.

Nothing would be much comfort, she thought dully.

Glancing at the bags containing her new dresses, she wondered if she could take them back. Maybe she'd try on Saturday. She had nothing else to do that day. Dusty wasn't coming on Friday. Would never be coming again. Not after what had happened.

Tears ran down her cheeks, but she didn't brush them away. She took another sip of brandy, a sob breaking as she tried to swallow. She was not going to have her weekend of dancing and breakfast in bed. It would be spent alone, like all the others. As would Christmas. Only this time she knew what she was missing. Carefully she placed the glass on a table and turned toward her bedroom. She was alone. She'd been alone all her life since her mother died. The time spent with her father had been the loneliest of all.

Until right now.

Dusty pulled into the yard and cut the engine. He glared through the windshield. The drive from Denver had done nothing to diminish his anger. Slamming his fist against the steering wheel, he cursed. He didn't know who he was maddest at—John for neglecting to read his damn mail for so long; Deb for leading him on all the time she lied; or himself for believing a single word she said.

His vote would go to himself. Dammit, he knew the kind of machinations business people pulled. Marjory used to gloat over shady deals. She gave "cutthroat" an entirely new meaning. Only she paled beside what Deb proved capable of.

He threw open the door and stormed into the house. He'd been played for a fool. Time to forget it and move on. It wouldn't be the first time, nor the last, most likely. He didn't treat people like that, and never had barriers up to deflect it. Next time he might be wiser, but somehow he doubted it. If a pretty woman told him blue, he'd believe it until her black heart proved him wrong.

At least Ms. Black-hearted, Scrooge Banker would have

some serious explaining to do to her boss. Dusty had pulled no punches when storming into that pompous idiot's office.

He strode down to his own office and flung his hat on the desk. Heading for the window, he gazed out over the fields his uncle had left him. It wasn't as if he hadn't known from the start that getting involved with a career woman was plain foolish. Hell, he was dumber than a stick if he thought Deb was going to be any different from Marjory. Her sob story for wanting security was probably just that, a story, made up to gain sympathy while she systematically continued her foreclosure process.

And now he had John all up on his high horse. Dammit, Dusty had the money; John could pay him back when he got on his feet again. John shouldn't have gone to the damn bank in the first place. But like most cattlemen, he had more pride than good sense.

Dusty stood by the window as night fell. He saw the lights in the bunkhouse, and in the barn. But he didn't move. Anger fed on itself and he constantly reviewed every lying word Deb Harrington had uttered. Even last night on the phone, she'd flirted and promised things he now knew she'd had no intention of delivering. Or had she thought he wouldn't learn of the foreclosure before the weekend? Had she wanted one weekend to flaunt all her flash and dash in his face, show off her fancy condo, her expensive foreign car? Too bad, he'd caught her out.

"Dusty?" Ivy asked from the doorway.

"What?"

"Missed you at supper." She flicked on a lamp. The soft glow did nothing to ease the darkness in Dusty's soul.

"Wasn't hungry."

"We heard about John," she said.

Dusty turned. "And?"

She shrugged and moved to straighten a cushion on a chair. "And you should have given him the money way back when, instead of him taking that bank loan. Never did trust banks."

"Or bankers," he growled.

She cocked her head. "What did Deb have to say about the situation?"

"Nothing."

"Nothing?"

He shook his head and dropped into his chair, bone weary.

"I can't believe she didn't have something to tell you about—"

"Leave it, Ivy. I didn't need her to tell me anything. I threw the papers in her face, told her I paid off the loan, and to stay the hell away from me. There was not one thing she had to say I wanted to hear."

"It just doesn't sound like Deb."

"What does it take to get you off a man's back? She's just like Marjory, for God's sake."

"Marjory? No, she's not like Marjory, Dusty. A blind man could see that."

"They're as alike as two peas in a pod, both so all-fired concerned with getting ahead, they don't care whom they trample in the rush."

"First—" Ivy touched her left index finger with her right "—Deb offered to help in the kitchen, more than once. In the year Marjory lived here she never once offered. Turned her nose up as if it were beneath her."

"Ivy—"

"Second, I think Deb is shy."

"Shy! Are you loco?"

Ivy continued as if Dusty hadn't spoken. "I suspected it at the barbecue, but she made a good effort, even mingling with the other women when we did the dishes. She made a genuine effort to fit in. Something Ms. Mighty Executive Marjory never did. And then at dinner after we found her on Sunday, she was grateful, and appreciative. She liked baking pies, asked a ton of questions. Dusty, she's not like Marjory."

He sighed, tipped back in his chair and waited for his house-keeper and cook to run down. Then he'd hustle her out and be done.

"Unlike Marjory, Deb liked the ranch. She watched everyone work, asked questions, even ventured out on her own, not demanding people keep her entertained.''

''And all the time she was delaying and stalling so she could present us with a fait accompli. Dammit, Ivy, I don't want to hear any more.''

''You're the boss.'' The older woman stood and smoothed down her jeans. ''A stubborn, opinionated, blind-as-a-bat, pig-headed male. Don't know why I try.''

''Close the door on your way out,'' he said.

''Want me to turn out the light?'' she asked, pausing by the door.

''No, I have work to do.''

''You should at least have asked her to explain,'' Ivy said as a parting shot.

Dusty listened to his friend's footsteps echo down the hall, heard the door close. Silence reigned.

''Some hurts go too deep, Ivy,'' he said slowly. ''Nothing can excuse them.''

Ten

Saturday morning Deb woke up angry. She'd gone past the bewilderment, past the confusion, and reached healthy, healing anger. The research she and Annalise had done yesterday answered all questions. The sadness was gone, her tears dried. She couldn't change things, but she could set the record straight with one smart-aleck, arrogant, know-it-all cowboy.

She pulled out her jeans, then shook her head and tossed them in the corner. This time she was going on her own terms. Pulling out a pair of brown, lightweight wool slacks, she donned them, then a pink silk blouse that complemented both the slacks and her complexion. She swept her hair into its usual French braid and applied a light touch of makeup.

Toast and coffee was all she wanted for breakfast. Without further delay, she hopped in to her car and headed west.

Her anger never eased as she drove the distance to the Wilson Ranch. She would set the record straight, get an apology, and return home. Maybe she'd swing by Barrett's to make sure he heard the true version. No sense leaving anything to chance. Obviously chance didn't play on her side.

Deb refused to let any other emotion enter. She would not enjoy the drive, even though the sky was a cloudless blue, the air coming in through the vents almost balmy and pine-scented. She would not enjoy the view of the Rockies, majestic and glorious in the morning sun. Nor permit a pang of nostalgia or yearning to creep in when she turned onto the road leading to the ranch house. Cold, controlled, and contained, those were her watchwords this morning. She would give Dusty the facts, and say goodbye.

Head held high, she turned into the ranch yard.

Two of the hands worked in the corral. They stopped and watched as she drove up and killed her engine. Neither raised a hand in greeting. Both stared at her, a look of disapproval visible on their faces even from the distance.

So be it. What she had to say would change that. Or maybe not, but she wouldn't know. She didn't plan to pass this way again.

Walking to the front door, Deb knocked. Waited. No one came. She heard no sounds inside the house. Glancing at her watch, Deb saw that it was after eleven. Dusty had been up long ago. She'd check the bunkhouse.

It felt funny to push open the door to the kitchen. Not knowing if she should knock or not, Deb peeked in. Ivy stood at the long counter, preparing lunch. A mammoth undertaking with all the cowhands and their hearty appetites.

"Hi, hon. Come on in. Want some coffee?" Ivy said, spying Deb at the door.

"I'm looking for Dusty."

"He's out and about. Be back for lunch. Want to wait?"

"Darn straight I do." Deb walked in, her head held so high she wondered if she would scrape the ceiling. If Ivy said one thing—

"Help yourself to coffee and set a spell. I'm just finishing lunch."

"Can I help?" The words spilled out involuntarily.

Ivy smiled and shook her head. "From time to time I might want some help, but I enjoy my work, and usually don't want anyone messing in my kitchen."

Deb nodded and fetched a cup of coffee. It was hot and strong, and gave her something to do with her hands. Sitting gingerly at the long table, she glanced around. Ruthlessly she clamped down on her memories, the emotions that churned. She held on to her anger. Once she said her piece, she'd leave. But she couldn't help the tiny bud of welcome she felt, the feeling of coming home.

"Come to set him straight, I reckon," Ivy murmured, trimming some of the ham before slicing it for more sandwiches. "Told him he should have asked you about it. I expect he slammed in and out before a body could think."

Deb nodded, her eyes on her coffee, watching the steam swirl in the sunlight.

"Men can be a pain sometimes," Ivy offered.

"All the time, as far as I can see," Deb replied, blinking hard to keep treacherous tears at bay. She'd cried all she planned to over Dusty Wilson. He wasn't worth it, no account, lazy— Well, maybe not lazy.

"He reminds me of my father," Deb said slowly.

"Do tell," Ivy said.

"Always charming his way through life, with no more sense of responsibility than a flea. Ne'er-do-wells who live by the skin of their teeth and their charm." And who don't mind who they hurt along life's way.

Ivy stopped and looked at Deb. "Are we talking about the same Dusty Wilson?"

Deb nodded. "You can't deny he's charming."

"As the angels. But, hon, Dusty Wilson is one of the hardest working men I've ever met."

"Come on, Ivy, I've seen this place. How hard does a man have to work to let it go to pot?"

"If he's sick with grief over the loss of his last child, he doesn't have to work too hard, hon. Dusty's uncle let this place fall almost to rack and ruin. Hank and I had already accepted jobs at another spread because Dusty's uncle was so broke he couldn't pay us another month. Heartsick he was. He doted on his son. It took several years, but when he died, the ranch teetered on the verge of bankruptcy. Dusty's turned this old place around in just over four years."

Deb looked up, skepticism clearly evident.

"You're looking at the main house that needs painting, not the miles of fencing that's all repaired, the gates that all hang properly, the feed for the beef, the healthy herd, the number of ranch hands it takes to run this place. And we're all paid well. More to a ranch than a painted house, hon."

The calluses on his palms. Suddenly she remembered the nagging point that had evaded her the other night. A man who dallied through life didn't have hardened calluses from work. His hands would be soft and smooth. Had she misjudged Dusty? Could he be different from her father?

"Do you think I deliberately led Dusty on while going behind his back to foreclose on John Barrett?" Deb asked, pushing the confusing thoughts away. She hadn't come to analyze her assessment of Dusty Wilson, she'd come to set the record straight.

Ivy looked at her for a long moment, then slowly shook her head. "Nope."

"Dusty does." Deb took a sip of coffee, annoyed at the sting of tears.

"Dusty's coming into this with a lot of baggage," Ivy said.

"Such as?"

"His ex-wife for one thing."

"Marjory."

"She would have done exactly what he thinks you did."

Deb had never had a chance. Every time Dusty looked at her, he saw his ex-wife. He never saw her, Deb, at all.

"Hey, Ivy, is lunch—" Hank entered, stopped dead when he saw Deb sitting at the table. His eyes narrowed, but before he could say anything, Ivy spoke.

"Hank, did Dusty ride back with you?"

"Yep."

"Where are the rest of the boys?"

"On their way."

Ivy turned to Deb. "Your best bet is to catch him in the barn. That is if you want to see him alone."

"Yes. Thanks for the coffee." Deb placed her cup in the sink and skirted Hank. Crossing to the barn, she passed three more of the men who worked the Wilson Ranch. Head high, she looked straight ahead, gave no sign she saw them. She felt their anger, their bitterness, the hard glances, but ignored it. Nothing could hurt her now.

The barn was redolent with the scent of fresh hay and warm horse. For a second the memory of their afternoon in the loft flashed into mind. Ruthlessly she pushed it away. Her anger simmered as she stalked toward the back of the huge building. Dusty stood beside Diego, brushing the big horse. He heard her footsteps and looked up. The dark anger on his face almost caused Deb to turn tail and run for her life. Almost, but not quite.

When she drew as close as she dared, she stopped and raked him from head to toe.

"Get out," Dusty said, turning back to curry Diego. His hand gripped the comb so tightly his knuckles turned white.

"Once I've had my say, I can't leave fast enough. But you will hear me out."

Dusty turned, resting one arm on Diego's back. His expression gave not a hint to his feelings. "I don't need to hear anything you have to say."

"You're wrong. You were wrong Thursday and you're wrong today, Dusty Wilson. I did not foreclose on John Barrett's loan. I am an honorable woman. I told you all along I couldn't guarantee anything, but I would hold off as long as I could so your neighbors could get the money together to bring the loan up to date. I would have told you when that time expired. I would have made sure you and John Barrett knew the next step was foreclosure."

"Yeah, well you talk a good talk, don't you? The way I see it, you stalled things long enough that all the paperwork was completed before I had a chance to do anything—like go over your head."

"Like you did Thursday?" she asked. "I hope you're pleased with that result. I never did one thing to hurt you, Dusty. I did everything I said. I didn't foreclose, Phil did."

"Phil? Who the hell is Phil?"

"Phil Moore. He is another loan officer at the bank, another one in line for the vice presidency. He and I don't exactly get along. Something alerted him to the fact I delayed a foreclosure. He took the file last week and processed it. The first I learned about it was when I read the papers you tossed on my desk."

He stared at her. "God," he said softly, when the full extent of what she'd said penetrated.

Deb wanted to smile as the expressions chased around his face, but her lips wobbled and tears filled her eyes. Clenching her fists, she tilted her chin. She would not cry in front of this man! She would not give him a clue as to how hurt she'd been—and still was!

"Deb—" He took a step toward her.

She flung up her hands as if blocking him, and stepped back. "I just wanted you to know the truth. I plan to stop by Mr. Barrett's house and let him know. I understand you don't think highly of me, but at least know that I'm not a liar."

"I'm sorry, Deb."

"Why should you be sorry? You never pretended to care anything for me. You were trying to save your friend. It was my misfortune to see more in our relationship than there was."

"What do you mean?" His eyes narrowed and he took another step closer, pausing just out of touching range.

"You accused me of stringing you along. Well, I think it's that you were stringing me along. Keep her happy, prevent her from foreclosing. And if I didn't fall in line, you could always go over my head to my boss. Which you threatened more than once, and then did—very effectively I might add."

Dusty swallowed and stepped closer, slowly, as if not to spook her. "I have a temper, it got out of hand on Thursday. I truly thought you had foreclosed. And I was so damned mad at the thought of you coming on to me just to keep me off your back—"

"Don't check your facts, right, Dusty? Is that the cowboy way? Plunge ahead and to hell with the consequences? A phone call, one question. I could have answered it for you. But not when you were yelling and throwing things, and not when I didn't have a clue what you were talking about.''

He took a deep breath. ''I thought you'd done it.''

''Because Marjory would have done it,'' she said sadly, knowing he saw his ex-wife every time he looked at her.

He went still. ''What do you know about Marjory?''

''Only that apparently I'm paying for her sins. I'm not Marjory. I don't know about her. But my sympathy is with her. I thought at first she must be a fool to divorce you. Now I see she was probably fighting for her life.''

''What are you talking about?'' If possible, his scowl had deepened.

''You don't like career women, you've made that abundantly clear. What wasn't made clear to me until Thursday is how vindictive you are. And why, Dusty? Do you have to be the top dog? Is it an ego thing? Why? According to Ivy, you're doing all right on this ranch, which you never bothered to show to me. You paid John's bill in full, as you said. You must be doing more than all right, since it wasn't a small loan. Why couldn't you allow me my one corner of the world? I never hurt you, Dusty. I—''

Deb stopped and turned. Slowly she started down the barn, resisting the strong urge to flee as if the hounds of hell pursued. She would leave before he saw the tears, with dignity—

Dusty's hand gripped her arm and spun her around.

''You love me, so you said.'' He leaned over her, his eyes dark and tormented. ''Right, Deb? You love me?''

She shook her head. ''No. I mistook passion for love. You're good in bed, you must know that. Another way to keep me in line?''

''For God's sake, Deb, I didn't do anything to keep you in line. I brought you out the first time to meet John. The rest, all of it after that first day, was just you and me. It had nothing to do with the loan, or the bank or anything.''

''So you say.''

''Dammit, it's the truth!''

''The truth is that if you cared anything for me as a person, much less a friend, you would have asked me about the fore-closure before storming the bank, and flinging those accusations in Mr. Montgomery's ear.''

"I'll go in and tell him it wasn't that way.''

She laughed bitterly, tears starting again. "It's too late.''

"What do you mean?''

She brushed the tears away, but they kept falling.

"Deb, honey, don't cry. Whatever is wrong, I'll fix it.'' He pulled her into his arms and held her tightly, resting his cheek on her soft hair.

"You already fixed it, Dusty. I'm no longer being considered as a vice president candidate. As far as the bank is concerned, I'm finished.''

He closed his eyes, his hands roaming over her in an attempt to soothe, but whether it was Deb he wanted to soothe or his own guilt, Dusty wasn't sure.

"There'll be other jobs,'' he said softly.

She pushed back and glared at him through her tears. "You still don't get it, do you? Even now. What if I yanked this ranch from you and sold it to someone else. Would you be placated with 'there are other ranches'?''

"It's not the same thing—''

"It is for me. Dusty, I didn't have much as a child, you already know that. I worked my tail off in college, getting good grades while working two part-time jobs. I landed a management trainee position with the bank and worked hard. For eight solid years, I've worked nights and weekends. My dream was to rise to be an officer in the bank. To have the respect and admiration of other people. You don't get much of that when you're living out of a car. That was my dream, Dusty. It wasn't yours, and you didn't even have to like it. But it was mine. And you trampled on it like it was dirt.''

"Deb, I didn't mean to—''

"Of course you did. Otherwise why wouldn't you see me before seeing Mr. Montgomery? You don't think a career is the right thing for a woman, so you saw a way to end it.''

He rubbed one hand over his face and stared down at her.

"Quit your job and come live here. I have enough work to keep you busy."

"What?"

"If you live here, you don't have to worry about the job at the bank, or promotion or living in Denver."

Deb couldn't believe her ears. Had he asked her before last Thursday, she would have been beside herself with joy. But not now. Rubbing her chest, she shook her head.

"You know, I've waited for love for a long time. Ever since my mama died. And I fell in love with you, Dusty, or rather with the charming man I thought I knew. But I didn't expect love to be so painful or hurtful. I didn't expect to find it's not something I want. I'm sure I'll get over you, you've gone a long way to helping in the cure. But the last person I'd want to tie my life with is you. And the last thing I want to do is give up my career." She almost spat the words.

"I want you, Deb."

"Is this your idea of atonement? Forget it! I like my job. I like working in a bank."

"You could work from here."

"Commute to Denver?" Why did she prolong the conversation? She would not marry him, though the ache in her chest grew stronger with each passing second. She had to leave.

"Get a job at a local bank. I don't know—we can work it out."

"My answer is no."

As he watched her walk from the barn, her head held high, Dusty knew his world had just ended. Her tears had touched something deep inside him. He'd hurt this pretty, young, vulnerable woman. Life had not been fair to her or easy. Because of his damnable temper, and because of Marjory, he'd just made it worse. Trust, once lost, was difficult if not impossible to regain. His anger and his blindness to her character had ruined anything between them.

Ivy had been right—Deb was not Marjory. But he hadn't seen that until now. As the full impact of her words hit, he felt as if he'd been pierced with a knife. He'd trampled her dream. She was right, it hadn't been his dream. Was he so arrogant he thought he should be the one to dictate people's dreams? And if they didn't go the way he wanted, ruthlessly cut them down? He couldn't be that insensitive. Not with a woman who meant more to him than anything.

He quickly walked to the open doors and watched as she climbed into her car. He wanted to stop her, but what could he say? He'd gone over her head and painted as bad a picture as he could. Anyone with half a mind would know it would have a serious impact on her career. God, he wished he could take back the words.

In only seconds the car had driven away. He had told himself over and over that she was like Marjory and he'd be a fool to fall for her. But he had anyway. He wanted Deb Harrington more than he wanted his next breath. The thought that she had played him for a fool was the trip wire to his temper on Thursday. To the temper that had simmered ever since. Until ten minutes ago.

He couldn't believe he'd stormed into her president's office and said the things he'd said. She was right, he should have asked her. But he'd been too hurt, too blinded by sheer painful rage, to think clearly.

And Deb had paid the price.

He knew how important her job was to her. If he were honest, he'd admit he was jealous. Jealous of the hours she spent on the job when she could be with him. Was it ego? Had he wanted Marjory to think he was wonderful, to need him to the exclusion of everything else? Had he resented time she spent at work? Was the same thing repeating itself with Deb?

There had to be a way to make things right for her. He wasn't sure exactly what it was, but he'd find it. He'd been wrong and hurt the one person he should never have hurt. He would have to find a way to make it up to her. Even then, he'd be lucky if she ever spoke to him. Had he shattered her love, just when he realized what a precious gift he'd found?

By the time Deb reached home Saturday night, she was exhausted. John Barrett had been cordial, actually friendly by the time she'd relayed the exact sequence of events. But the emotions of the day had drained her.

A message waited on her machine from Dusty. She erased it and fixed herself soup for dinner. Sunday morning, she started in on a résumé. Working on it all day, she was marginally satisfied by the time she went to bed. Her phone rang several times, but she unhooked the machine and ignored the ringing.

Monday, Deb arrived at the bank exactly on time. No more coming in early for her. She would call a headhunter today and begin to look for another position. Her future at this bank had ended.

Annalise was on the phone. When she spotted Deb, she stopped talking, doodling on her notepad until Deb entered her office. As Deb put away her handbag, she caught Annalise looking in, then looking away, talking hurriedly, quietly, on the phone.

Color stained Deb's cheeks. Gossip, probably, about what happened last week. Well, she had done nothing wrong. She thought Annalise was on her side, but maybe the temptation to discuss the situation proved too much for her assistant. She would ignore her, and get out of this place as soon as she found something new.

The day dragged by. She had no enthusiasm left for her projects. And she hated Phil's smirks when she passed him in the hallway. She had a meeting scheduled tomorrow with a headhunter. Hopefully a new job would turn up soon.

Deb was late returning from lunch on Tuesday. Her meeting to discuss career options had gone well and the headhunter thought he'd be able to line up several opportunities for her to choose among. Annalise pounced the moment she arrived.

"Deb, Mr. Montgomery has been calling for you for almost half an hour. You'd better go right there."

"What does he want, do you know?" Deb asked, wondering if she would be fired outright if she refused the summons. How much more could he want to berate her?

"I don't know, but he sounded impatient the last time he called."

"Okay. I'll drop my purse and head for the inner sanctum."

The president's secretary rose and ushered Deb into Mr. Montgomery's office. Deb was startled to see Dusty sitting in one of the visitor's chairs. A Dusty she scarcely recognized. His hair had been trimmed and lay neatly combed. He wore a dark business suit that fit as if it had been designed for him, a crisp, snowy-white shirt and a sleek maroon-and-silver tie. He looked the epitome of a successful businessman—and like he'd never even seen a horse or steer.

"You wanted to see me, Mr. Montgomery?" she said, standing near the door, warily watching the two men.

"Come in, Deb, my dear. Come in and have a seat. I know I don't need to introduce William Wilson to you, now do I?" Montgomery laughed heartily and motioned her to the second visitor's chair.

Deb looked at Dusty. *William Wilson?*

"Hello, sweetheart, sorry I missed you for lunch. We'll have to catch up on everything over dinner."

Deb said nothing as she took the offered chair, looking between her boss and the baffling man who sat beside her.

"William explained to me about the mix-up last week. Sorry about that Deb. You should have set me straight."

Deb looked at Dusty—what was going on?

Dusty smiled easily. "If I hadn't been out of town when Dusty left the ranch, none of this would have happened. I've spoken to his nurse. He'll make sure Dusty doesn't get away like that again. You understand, Josiah, it's difficult, and an embarrassment to the family. We try to keep things under wraps."

"Sure, William, I think we can manage that. You know banks are known for confidential handling of client information."

Had she fallen into wonderland? She hadn't a clue what was going on.

"As you may be aware, Josiah, Deb has one little quirk— she freezes when there's yelling. Had Dusty not been loud and obnoxious, threatening even, she could have gotten to the bottom of the situation without all the hassles.''

''Yes, you mentioned that. All water under the bridge. Now, to business.'' Leaning back in his high-backed executive chair, Mr. Montgomery smiled at Deb. ''Looks like we have a promotion in the works.''

''We do?'' She knew she had to be dreaming. She couldn't ever remember Mr. Montgomery smiling at her. And how had Dusty come to call him by his first name?

''She doesn't know?'' Montgomery looked at Dusty.

He shook his head, avoiding looking at Deb. ''This is business, Josiah. Thought I should discuss it with you first.''

''Well, well, I'm delighted to tell you, Deb, we have a new client at the bank. And they have asked specifically for you. Naturally the account is too large for a mere manager to handle. So I'm pleased to offer you the position of vice president, effective the end of the month when Harry March retires.''

Deb stared at him. ''Could you explain that a bit?'' From almost being fired last Thursday to the coveted promotion less than a week later seemed fantastic. She had to be dreaming. Any minute she'd wake up.

''A certain ball club is moving their account to the bank—investments, operating capital, payroll, everything. They will do this only if you are on board as the contact they can deal with. Your reputation is sterling, and they asked for you.'' Mr. Montgomery beamed at her as if she were his favorite child.

''I see,'' Deb replied, not understanding a word. She looked at Dusty. He looked back, his blue eyes dark and unfathomable. She didn't understand anything except he'd somehow gotten her the coveted promotion.

Slowly, Deb rose. ''Thank you, Mr. Montgomery. May I let you know my decision tomorrow?''

''What? Don't you know what I've offered?'' The familiar scowl dropped back into place as he leaned forward obviously astonished she'd even hesitate.

''Indeed I do. Thank you. I'll let you know tomorrow.''

Deb fixed her glare on Dusty. "Maybe you'd like to walk me back to my office, *William*."

"Talk to her, my boy," Josiah Montgomery said gruffly.

Dusty nodded as he rose. "I'll fix things, Josiah. Good to meet you." The men shook hands warmly as Deb waited impatiently by the door.

Leading the way, she walked quickly to her office, glaring at Annalise's guilty expression. Once Dusty entered, she closed the door firmly behind them.

"Want to explain that scene?" she asked, leaning against her solid wooden door, afraid her legs wouldn't hold long enough to cross to her desk.

Dusty turned and smiled that charming, lopsided smile that melted her insides. "Which part?"

"All of it. Start with how you and *Josiah* got to be so chummy."

"Man thing, sweetcakes. When I explained the problem of my brother, and apologized profusely, of course Josiah was all that was gracious. Well, that might be a stretch, but he thawed a bit."

"Your brother? Which brother?"

"My twin, Dusty."

"Dusty, you didn't." The pain of the last several days diminished a degree as she took in the full ramifications of what he implied.

"If you think I dressed up this fine to just jaw with the man, you're nuts. I had to look as different as I could, and act different, too. That way he bought my story about my deranged twin brother, Dusty—who goes off his head sometimes, accusing people of the weirdest things. I heard he let loose in the bank last week and so I wanted to stop by and set things right."

A giggle bubbled up. Deb tried to stop it but couldn't. "I wish I could have seen Mr. Montgomery's face. I can't believe you did it. Or that Montgomery believed you."

"Hey, I look trustworthy, and rich."

She assessed his suit, the discreet gold watch on his wrist, the styled hair. "I guess you do, and money talks."

"That's what bankers think, sweetcakes. And it works. So does good old-fashioned bribery."

"The ball club?"

"Yeah."

"How in the world—"

Dusty took a step closer, reaching out to rest his hands on her shoulders. "The owner is a friend of my dad's. A good friend. I asked a huge favor, made some promises, and agreed to supply the team with steak for the rest of my life. Do you know how much steak athletes can eat?"

She shook her head, unable to think. He stood too close. He always short-circuited her thought process just being near. She wanted to lean in against him, to soak up his strength, to feel for a few moments as if she wasn't so alone. She held herself stiff. She would not give in to this man again. She'd learned that lesson well.

He leaned over until his forehead almost touched hers. "I wanted to make up for the wrong I did, sweetcakes. This was the only way I could find."

She pushed out of his arms and walked to her desk, fiddling with a pencil there. "I don't think I can take the promotion. It's not based on my work, only on the bribe you're bringing. I wanted to get the promotion based on merit, not bribery."

"Deb, are you qualified for the position?" he asked.

She nodded. "Yes, I believe so."

"More so than Phil?"

She looked over at him. "Definitely!"

"Then if you want to play with the big boys, you need to learn to play hardball. And this is a business coup that will keep you employed for years. Look on these last few days as an aberration. You are back on track now."

"Am I?"

"Listen to me, Deb. My temper got away and I did something I'll always regret—I hurt you. I knocked things off track, but now I'm hoping I put them back. One thing this whole mess accomplished, however, was to show me how much I care for you. I thought part of me died when you cried in the barn. Between you and Ivy, I've realized a lot of things lately.

First is that you are Deb Harrington, no one else. You are not Marjory. I saw similarities, but that's all they were—a few similarities. You are unique, and I overlooked that for a while. If you can't forgive what I've done, I'll have to learn to live with it, won't I? But I think you're generous enough to give me another chance.''

Just then a sharp rap came on the door and it opened. Annalise stood in the opening. "Is everything all right here?" she asked suspiciously, glaring at Dusty.

"Yes, but thank you for coming to my rescue." Deb smiled at her assistant. "Dusty's leaving."

Annalise stepped farther into the office, and out of the doorway. She watched as Dusty hesitated, then nodded.

"I'll be in touch."

Deb said nothing, watching as he left. She felt numb. She'd had no warning of what awaited her return from lunch and didn't know how to feel.

"Are you really all right?" Annalise asked.

"Yes, I think I am." Slowly Deb walked around her desk and sat down. "Thanks for checking on me."

"After last Thursday, the last thing I thought you would want was to be alone in the office with a madman," Annalise replied.

Deb nodded, gazing off into space. She had a lot to think about, and not much time to make some important decisions.

Impulsively she jumped up. Taking her purse, she smiled at Annalise. "I'm taking the rest of the day off. Handle anything that comes up."

"Deb? Are you ill?"

"No, just taking a few hours for myself. See you in the morning."

For the first time since she started work, Deb walked out of the bank hours before the day ended. The sunshine shone bright, warming her cheeks as she strolled the sidewalks. The air felt almost like springtime instead of December.

She had nothing to do this afternoon but decide her entire future.

Eleven

Deb felt pleasantly tired when she returned home. She'd walked for a while, ending up in the park in front of the state capitol. It had been years since she'd taken an afternoon off just to sit in a park. She enjoyed it.

She kicked off her high heels, promising herself to carry flats if she planned any more walking afternoons, and headed for the bedroom. A knock at the door stopped her. She rarely had visitors. But she couldn't help the leap in her heart as she headed for the door.

Opening it, she stared at the man. Cowboy, pure and simple—rugged as the Old West, hard as the Colorado Rockies. From freshly polished but rather worn cowboy boots, up new jeans held with a bright shiny silver buckle, up to the wide shoulders and strong neck, to the pugnacious jaw, her heart rate increased as her eyes inched up the hard face. His hat rode so low she could scarcely see his eyes. Fascinated, she stared at it. It was new, decorated with holly at the band and as red as a fire engine! What in the world was he up to?

Gripping the doorknob like a lifeline, she remained silent.

The ball was in his court. She wondered what he would say, wondered why he had come.

Dusty watched the door open. Deb held on to the knob and stared at him. Nervous, he cleared his throat. Obviously she wasn't going to make this easy. Hell, he didn't blame her. "I'm a bit late for Friday's dinner, but I'm here."

Her eyes widened and his heart dropped. Was she going to slam the door in his face? He glanced at the jamb. Could he get his boot in the way to keep the door open if she moved? Afraid to spook her, he remained still.

He brought his hand out from behind his back, bringing a huge bouquet of ruby-red roses and dainty white baby's breath he had scoured the downtown area for. He held the flowers out to her, watching closely to try to gauge her reaction. Something eased inside him at the obvious surprise and delight that exploded when she saw the flowers. Her smile warmed his heart. The cold dissipated a bit.

"Dusty, they're beautiful!"

"They are not as pretty as you are," he said, struck anew by her soft beauty.

Tears filled her eyes as she smiled at the bouquet. "No one ever gave me flowers before," she murmured quietly.

Dusty hoped the flowers were a start. He shifted on the stoop.

"Come in and I'll put them in water." She turned and headed for the kitchen, her stocking feet silent on the floor, his boots resounding as he followed close behind her. The first step was made—he was in!

Deb felt flustered. She wasn't sure what to do, so to stall for time, she busied herself arranging the flowers in a vase. The heady fragrance of the roses filled the kitchen, and filled her heart. Any idiot knew what red roses meant. Didn't Dusty?

"Why in the world are you wearing a red hat?" she asked as she fussed with the blossoms, trying to display every single one to best advantage.

"It's almost Christmas. It's festive, don't you think?" he

asked, turning it in his hand. It looked silly, now. But he'd bought it with the thought of making her laugh, to take away some of the aching hurt that had been in her eyes the last time he'd seen her.

"Yes, I think it looks very festive," she said gravely, looking at the hat. "Why did you come, Dusty? Or is it William?" she said, peeping at him from beneath her lashes.

He smiled and Deb's heart flip-flopped. Her knees grew weak and she wondered if she could remain standing.

"I came to take you to dinner. Maybe dancing, if you feel like it."

Deb took in the tall cowboy standing there, twirling that bright red hat, dressed up and raring to go. Her heart quickened. Then she thought of all the walking she'd done that afternoon and shook her head. "No dancing tonight, thank you. Would you like to eat here? I could fix something."

"I don't care, I just want to be with you. I hoped you would let me stay."

She studied him suspiciously. This didn't sound like the Dusty she knew. Even given everything that had happened, he sounded too subdued, too somber for Dusty Wilson. She would have expected him to try to charm his way in, explain away his behavior and lazily demand she let him stay.

"And that's all?" she asked, walking so close she almost touched him, tilting her head back until she could gaze into his eyes. "Just to be with me?"

He hesitated for a single second. Tossing his hat onto the table, he pulled her into his arms and crushed her. "Hell, no that's not all. I want much more, starting with every little bit of you." His mouth came down and the earth spun around. Deb clutched his broad chest and hung on. The ride would be glorious.

He slanted his mouth for better access, deepened his kiss. Deb returned the embrace, her tongue dancing with his, teasing, coaxing, tantalizing; her hands touching, petting, provoking until they were both burning with longings and desire. Dusty's hard hands caressed her, molded her body to his as if he couldn't get enough of her, couldn't get her close enough. Still Deb pressed closer.

"You're right, I don't want to go out to eat," he said against her throat, his hot lips trailing fire over every inch of exposed skin. "I want to eat you up right here and now." His mouth closed over hers again and Deb stopped thinking. She could only feel. She missed him, felt as if her heart had shattered into tiny bits. But the obvious desire he made no effort to hold in check was a soothing balm that healed every ragged edge.

All afternoon, she'd thought about Dusty and their relationship, but she had never expected to see him so soon. She tightened her arms, and returned every stroke, every caress. She wanted this man more than anything. He had to want her as much. He couldn't be holding her this tightly if he didn't, he couldn't be loving her this well if he didn't. Or was she living in some idiotic dream? Would she waken to find herself alone once again?

"My bedroom is down the hall," she whispered when he trailed hot kisses up her neck to nip lightly on her ear. If this were a dream, she wanted it to be the best one she ever had.

"Allow me." He picked her up and the room whirled. Feeling as sexy and glamorous as a film star, Deb smiled in pure delight as she clung to her amorous cowboy. Dusty looked uncomfortable when he slowly set her on her feet beside the feminine coverlet of the canopy bed. He glanced around the room, then back to Deb. "It looks like you—sweet and soft and so feminine, I feel as clumsy as a bull."

She traced her fingertips across his rugged jaw. "The bed is sturdy, and so am I," she said, a shy smile lighting her features. "I still want you."

"Oh, sweetcakes, I want you more than life."

In a flurry of hands and fingers, their clothes were discarded. If it took longer with each helping the other, it only added to the spicy anticipation that built as palms caressed, lips kissed and skin heated.

Tumbling together into bed, they clung together, silent for

a moment, still, each savoring the familiar heated feel of the other.

"We have to talk, you know," Dusty said, nuzzling that sensitive spot behind her ear.

"Now?" Deb asked. She was a shimmering mass of feelings and sensation. She could no more carry on a conversation than she could ride a bull.

"If you could talk now, I'm doing something wrong," he murmured, his thumb gently stroking a taut nipple.

She shook her head, tasting his skin as he moved over her. "We can talk later."

"Much later," he agreed as his tongue teased her, as his hands sensitized every nerve ending.

He brought her again and again to the shining precipice, but Deb refused to go over alone. She'd been alone too much in her life; it was time to share. Daringly, she traced his muscles, teased his nipples, nipped his shoulder, until his pace was as frantic as hers. Then she urged him higher. She loved Dusty Wilson, and she wanted to express that love every way she could. Once and for all that man would know how she felt. If he could grow to love her, she would die a happy woman. If not, she at least had the fleeting joy of the night.

When they crashed over the top together, Deb knew she'd never experienced anything as glorious. Unable to breathe, unable to think, she could only feel the sizzling contractions expand until her whole world comprised Dusty, and ecstasy and delight.

"Deb?" he said softly sometime later. It was dark, quiet, peaceful.

"Mmm?"

"Are you awake?"

"Mmm." She snuggled closer to the hard chest that cushioned her head. Her arm flung around his waist, she let her fingers rub against his taut skin.

"Want to eat, or talk?"

"Neither," she murmured. She just wanted to float forever.

"I want to eat, then talk, then maybe come back to bed."

"Let's skip the first two and stay right here," she said dreamily.

"I need to make sure we've cleared the air. That things are all right between us again," Dusty said. "And I haven't had anything to eat since breakfast. After this workout, I'm hungry."

Deb slowly pulled back. She scooted up to the headboard and plumped a pillow. Drawing the sheet to cover her breasts, she tucked it beneath her arms and looked at him. The room was dim. But she didn't want to turn on a light. She liked the twilight—it was soft, forgiving.

"I can fix something or we could order in," she said, running her hands through her hair.

Dusty sighed and started to get out of bed. "I vote for pizza. I'll call, if you like. Is there a place close by that delivers?"

"Yes." She watched as he pulled on his jeans, stomped into his boots. When he buttoned his shirt, she wanted to stop him. But her apartment was cool and it might just be fun to take it off him later. She smiled in anticipation. "The number is in the front of the phone book."

When Dusty left to call in their order, Deb rose and rummaged through her closet for something very feminine to wear. Dusty normally saw her in her business suits or the jeans she wore to his ranch. She wanted—ah, here it was. A filmy caftan. Perfect. The color blended blues and rose. She slipped it over her body, still sensitive from Dusty's touch. The cool cotton caressed her skin. She moved and savored the feel. She found her slippers and put them on. The caftan covered them when she walked.

Brushing her hair, she stared at her reflection. Was that dazzling smile hers? Were those sparkling eyes with a hint of mysterious satisfaction in their depths really hers? She sprayed a mist of perfume and turned to straighten the bed before she left the room.

Dusty was in her living room, building a fire in her fireplace. He had switched on the lights to the Christmas tree, their soft colors reflecting the soft love in her heart.

"Did you order the pizza?" she asked.

He nodded, turning to glance her way. Slowly he rose, never taking his eyes off her. "That's real pretty," he said gruffly.

Deb smiled and floated to him. Tilting her face, she met his kiss with her own rising passion. If they didn't stop, they would be otherwise occupied when the pizza arrived. Gently she pulled back.

"That's nice. I don't often have a fire," she said, trying to catch her breath.

"I figured as much with these store-bought logs. The pizza will be here in another ten minutes."

He reached for her hand and fiddled with her fingers. "We could sit on the sofa until the food arrives."

"Sure." She led the way, but once he sat down, she scooted so close she was practically in his arms. Resting her head on his shoulder, she gazed into the fire.

Dusty took a deep breath. He couldn't skirt the issue forever. He was surprised she'd even let him in. "I'm sorry about last week, Deb. If you want, I'll get you a two-by-four and you can whomp me upside the head the next time I go off on a tear like that."

"There won't be a next time," she said.

He caught his breath, the pain piercing. "There won't?" He could scarcely get the words out. Was she sending him away? Didn't she want to see him again?

"I don't think so."

"Meaning?" He waited for the ax to fall.

"Meaning you won't go off like that again," she said simply.

"I won't?"

"Dusty, I hurt your feelings when I compared you to my dad, but that was because I didn't know you well enough to know the difference. You hurt me when you went over my head and blasted my reputation with my boss. But that's because you didn't know the difference between me and Marjory. Now I hope you do. I know you better. I think if we work at it, we could get to know each other very well. And if so, misunderstandings, anger, things like that, will be reduced. Don't you think?"

"I guess." He thought a minute. "I was out of line big-time last week, and I can guarantee you it won't ever happen again. About your job—if you like working in a bank, go for it. I won't stand in your way, nor snipe at it anymore. What you said in the barn Saturday made me see how unfair I'd been. I superimposed my problems with Marjory onto you. The two of you are nothing alike. I know that. I knew it all along, but I was afraid to trust myself with a woman again. Especially a career woman."

She rubbed his shoulder with her cheek, the emotions grow-ing in her until she could scarcely sit still. She had not ex-pected this. Never thought to see Dusty change his views for her.

"I don't like the idea of your commute, but I can live with it, if you can," he said.

She looked into his eyes at those words, lost in the heat that blazed. "What?"

"I love you, Deb. You said once you loved me. If you can again one day, I'd like us to get married. I'll have the ranch, you'll have the bank. The commute will be hellacious, but if you keep the condo, I'll come in a couple of days during the week so you don't have to drive out all the time. We can work something out."

"I thought you had something against career women." Her heart beat so fast he had to notice. Blood pounded in her ears, almost deafening her. Hope blossomed, grew.

"Not when she's my very own. What about you? Thought you didn't like cocky ne'er-do-wells."

"I don't, but I love charming ranchers who work hard and cover it up with a lackadaisical attitude that could sure fool a stranger."

"Not ranchers, darling, just one."

"Just one," she agreed, her eyes soft with love.

"I'm sorry about last week. I'll spend the rest of my life trying to make it up to you. I know once trust is lost, it's hard to recapture."

She placed her finger over his lips. "I think you made it up today. Do you really think I can accept that vice president slot?"

"Yes, I truly think you should. And by holding out until tomorrow, Josiah will probably raise the salary a bit. He wants that account."

She laughed, leaning her head against his shoulder.

"What's so funny?"

"I'm just picturing you at bank picnics and Christmas parties. You'll be William Wilson with the deranged twin for the rest of our lives."

Dusty closed his eyes and smiled. "It's a small price to pay to have a 'rest of our lives.' I love you, sweetcakes."

"I love you, William Dusty Wilson. I always will."

"Might as well do this right," he muttered. "Wait right there. A man can't do important things without his hat." In two seconds he was back, the red Stetson riding back on his head. He knelt beside the sofa and took her hand in his.

"Deb Harrington, I love you. Would you do me the very great honor of marrying me?" He looked into her eyes and saw the love that shone from her soul—and the tears that welled. He hadn't made her sad, had he? He thought she loved him enough to join her life with his. God, he hadn't made another mistake, had he?

She swallowed and nodded, smiling even as the tears ran down her cheeks. "Dusty Wilson, the honor would be all mine. Yes, I will marry you." She pulled her hand free and flung her arms around his neck, slipping off the sofa to land in his lap.

The kiss that sealed their love blasted away the last of the hurt and anger. Their love had made it through the crucible, had survived and been strengthened. The future looked as bright as a new Christmas ornament.

The doorbell interrupted.

When Dusty uttered a short oath, Deb giggled and moved to let him get up. "You were the one who was hungry," she reminded him.

"Delivery people should have better timing," he muttered as he headed for the door.

They sat in front of the fire. Deb brought out beer and napkins and they ate directly from the box, sharing smiles, touching from time to time.

"Will you mind spending Christmas with my family? It's a pretty large gathering, and Ivy thinks you're a bit shy. But they're going to want to meet the woman I'm marrying right away," Dusty said later when they were almost finished.

Visions of large family gatherings filled her head and her heart. She'd need to buy presents, make cookies. For a moment shyness held sway, but she batted the feeling away. She would be with Dusty. Strengthened by his love, she could face anything. And why wouldn't his family be as friendly as the hands on the ranch? They loved him, and so did she.

"The only thing is," he continued, "I'm not quite sure how to introduce you. I find it kind of hard to think of you as a hard-hearted banker or Scrooge anymore. What will that do to your image?"

She smiled at his teasing, relaxed and secure in his love. "I think it will survive. Besides, it would have been blasted pretty soon anyway. Mommies are never Scrooge-like."

"Mommies!" Dusty dropped his pizza, his startled gaze fastening on hers. "Are you telling me—"

"Nothing yet, but one day soon, don't you think? Neither of us is exactly a kid. And if you want a houseful of babies, we'd better get started soon."

"You're right, sweetcakes." He dumped the rest of the pizza back into the box and swooped down to pick her up. "Time's awasting."

She laughed, her heart bubbling with happiness. "Dusty, I love you."

"I only hope as much as I love you," he said as he carried her back to their bedroom and closed the door on the past. No matter what the future held, they could face it together—with love.

* * * * *

Watch for Barbara McMahon's sexy new duet about twin sisters—coming the Spring of 1999, only from Silhouette Desire®

SILHOUETTE

Desire

COMING NEXT MONTH

THE PASSIONATE G-MAN Dixie Browning

Man of the Month/Lawless Heirs

Daniel Lawless was hiding out, a secret agent double-crossed by his own agency. Then Jasmine Clancy stumbled upon him and his life got even *more* complicated. Now he had to protect Jasmine too—and try to deny the passion between them—at least for now...

HOW TO HOOK A HUSBAND (AND A BABY) Carolyn Zane

Daddy Knows Last

Determined to be married by thirty, Wendy Wilcox begged her hunky neighbour Travis Donovan for some tips on seduction. But after the steamy 'pretend' kisses they shared, she had to admit she'd already found her ideal groom!

SEDUCING THE PROPER MISS MILLER Anne Marie Winston

Everyone said that black sheep, Thad Shippen, was not the sort of man for Miss Chloe Miller. But Chloe knew he was meant to be her husband, because this man they said was all bad, was oh, so good for her...

JUST A LITTLE BIT PREGNANT Eileen Wilks

The doctor had confirmed it—Jacy James was two months pregnant. Her twelve-hour affair with Tom Rasmussin had apparently left her more than just satisfied. But the trouble was Tom had disappeared before the sheets were even cold...

THE BODYGUARD AND THE BRIDESMAID Metsy Hingle

Right Bride, Wrong Groom

Protecting people was Ryan Fitzpatrick's job—but being Clea Mason's bodyguard was going to be pure pleasure. And the best way for Ryan to keep her safe was by pretending to be her husband.

THE TEXAN Catherine Lanigan

When Rafe met Angela he welcomed another *temporary* affair. Until Angela said two little words: *I'm pregnant*. Then he proposed, but Angela wasn't going to say yes unless Rafe could turn himself into a suitable groom...

COMING NEXT MONTH FROM

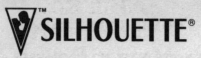 **SILHOUETTE**®

Sensation

A thrilling mix of passion, adventure and drama

POSSESSION Maura Seger
GUARDING JEANNIE Beverly Barton
THE HUSBAND SHE COULDN'T REMEMBER Maggie Shayne
RYDER'S WIFE Sharon Sala

Intrigue

Danger, deception and desire

A NEW YEAR'S CONVICTION Cassie Miles
EASY LOVING Sheryl Lynn
DECEIVING DADDY Susan Kearney
THE MAN THAT GOT AWAY Harper Allen

Special Edition

Satisfying romances packed with emotion

MARRIAGE BY NECESSITY Christine Rimmer
STALLION TAMER Lindsay McKenna
BELOVED MERCENARY Helen R. Myers
NATURAL BORN TROUBLE Sherryl Woods
STAY... Allison Leigh
HE'S GOT HIS DADDY'S EYES Lois Faye Dyer

JoAnn Ross
Anne Stuart
Margot Dalton

NEW YEAR'S RESOLUTION:
BABY

Welcome the New Year with this festive
collection of stories about romantic new
year celebrations and the gorgeous babies
who give their families an extra special
reason to celebrate!

Three original stories in one volume by
three star authors.

There must be something in the water in the little town of New Hope, there are certainly a lot of babies on the way! In this exciting new series, meet five delighted Mums-to-be. And the handsome hunks who get some surprising news...

Starting next month with:

THE BABY NOTION
Dixie Browning
DESIRE October 1998

Followed by:

BABY IN A BASKET
Helen R. Myers
DESIRE November 1998

MARRIED...WITH TWINS!
Jennifer Mikels
SPECIAL EDITION December 1998

HOW TO HOOK A HUSBAND (AND A BABY)
Carolyn Zane
DESIRE January 1999

DISCOVERED: DADDY
Marilyn Pappano
SENSATION February 1999

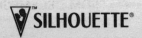

SHARON
SALA

Tory Lancaster is a woman trying to
leave behind a legacy of abandonment and sorrow.
She is about to come face to face with her past. A past
she must confront if she is to have any
hope of possessing a future.

SWEET
BABY

1-55166-416-X
**AVAILABLE IN PAPERBACK
FROM DECEMBER, 1998**

RACHEL LEE

CAUGHT

Someone is stalking and killing women, someone with
a warped obsession. And with loving devotion the
stalker has chosen Kate Devane as his next victim.
What he hasn't realised is that Kate is not alone. She
has a lover. A lover she has never met.

*Rachel Lee takes readers on a "sensational journey
into Tami Hoag/Karen Robards territory."*
—Publishers Weekly

MIRA®

1-55166-298-1
**AVAILABLE IN PAPERBACK
FROM NOVEMBER, 1998**

4 FREE

books and a surprise gift!

We would like to take this opportunity to thank you for reading this Silhouette® book by offering you the chance to take FOUR more specially selected titles from the Desire™ series absolutely FREE! We're also making this offer to introduce you to the benefits of the Reader Service™—

- ★ FREE home delivery
- ★ FREE gifts and competitions
- ★ FREE monthly newsletter
- ★ Books available before they're in the shops
- ★ Exclusive Reader Service discounts

Accepting these FREE books and gift places you under no obligation to buy; you may cancel at any time, even after receiving your free shipment. Simply complete your details and return the entire page to the address below. *You don't even need a stamp!*

YES! Please send me 4 free Desire books and a surprise gift. I understand that unless you hear from me, I will receive 6 superb new titles every month for just £2.50 each, postage and packing free. I am under no obligation to purchase any books and may cancel my subscription at any time. The free books and gift will be mine to keep in any case.

D8YE

Ms/Mrs/Miss/Mr...................................Initials ....
BLOCK CAPITALS PLEASE

Surname ....

Address ....

....

....Postcode..................................

Send this whole page to:
THE READER SERVICE, FREEPOST CN81, CROYDON, CR9 3WZ
(Eire readers please send coupon to: P.O. BOX 4546, DUBLIN 24.)

Offer not valid to current Reader Service subscribers to this series. We reserve the right to refuse an application and applicants must be aged 18 years or over. Only one application per household. Terms and prices subject to change without notice. Offer expires 30th June 1999. You may be mailed with offers from other reputable companies as a result of this application. If you would prefer not to share in this opportunity please write to The Data Manager at the address shown above.

Silhouette Desire is a registered trademark used under license.

LINDA HOWARD

DIAMOND BAY

Someone wanted this man dead. He was barely alive as
he floated up to the shore. Shot twice and unconscious.
Rachel's sixth sense told her she was his only hope.
The moment she decided not to call the police
she decided his future. As well as her own.

"Howard's writing is compelling."

—Publishers Weekly

1-55166-307-4
**AVAILABLE IN PAPERBACK
FROM DECEMBER, 1998**